✔ KU-024-264

The Dare Game

Jacqueline Wilson

Illustrated by Nick Sharratt

CORGI YEARLING

THE DARE GAME
A CORGI YEARLING BOOK : 9780440868200

First published in Great Britain by Doubleday
an imprint of Random House Children's Books

Doubleday edition published 2000
First Corgi Yearling edition published 2001
This Corgi Yearling edition published 2006

3 5 7 9 10 8 6 4

Copyright © Jacqueline Wilson, 2000
Illustrations copyright © Nick Sharratt, 2000

The right of Jacqueline Wilson to be identified as the author of this work has been
asserted in accordance with the Copyright, Designs and Patents Act 1988.

All rights reserved. No part of this publication may be reproduced, stored in a retrieval system,
or transmitted in any form or by any means, electronic, mechanical, photocopying, recording
or otherwise, without the prior permission of the publishers.

The Random House Group Limited supports The Forest Stewardship
Council (FSC), the leading international forest certification organisation.
All our titles that are printed on Greenpeace approved FSC certified paper
carry the FSC logo. Our paper procurement policy can be found at:
www.rbooks.co.uk/environment.

Corgi Yearling Books are published by Random House Children's Books,
61–63 Uxbridge Road, London W5 5SA,
A Random House Group Company.

Addresses for companies within The Random House Group Limited
can be found at: www.randomhouse.co.uk/offices.htm

THE RANDOM HOUSE GROUP Limited Reg. No. 954009
www.kidsatrandomhouse.co.uk

A CIP catalogue record for this book is available from the British Library.

Printed and bound in Great Britain by
Cox & Wyman Ltd, Reading, Berkshire

To Jessie Atkinson
Francesca Oates
Zoe
Lee and Sarah
Emma Walker and all my friends at
Redriff School
and everyone else who ever wondered
what happened to Tracy Beaker

No Home

You know that old film they always show on the telly at Christmas, *The Wizard of Oz*? I love it, especially the Wicked Witch of the West with her cackle and her green face and all her special flying monkeys. I'd give anything to have a wicked winged monkey as an evil little pet. It could whiz through the sky, flapping its wings and sniffing the air for that awful stale instant-coffee-and-talcum-powder *teacher* smell and then it would s-w-o-o-p straight onto Mrs Vomit Bagley and carry her away screaming.

That'll show her. I've always been absolutely Tip Top at writing stories, but since I've been at this stupid new school Mrs V.B. just puts '*Disgracefully untidy work, Tracy*' and '*Check your spellings!*' Last week we had to write a story about 'Night-time' and I thought it an unusually cool subject so I wrote eight and a half pages about this girl out late at night and it's seriously spooky and then this crazy guy jumps out at her and almost murders her but she escapes by jumping in the river and then she swims right into this bloated corpse and *then* when she staggers onto the bank there's this strange flickering light coming from the nearby graveyard and it's an evil occult sect wanting to sacrifice an innocent young girl and she's *just* what they're looking for . . .

It's a truly GREAT story, better than any that Cam could write. (I'll tell you about Cam in a minute.) I'm sure it's practically good enough to get published. I typed it out on Cam's computer so it looked ever so neat and the spellcheck took care of all the spellings so I was all prepared for Mrs V.B. to bust a gut and write: '*Very very very good indeed, Tracy. 10 out of 10 and Triple Gold Star and I'll buy you a tube of Smarties at playtime.*'

Do you know what she really wrote? '*You've tried hard, Tracy, but this is a very rambling story. You also have a very warped imagination!*'

I looked up 'warp' in the dictionary she's always recommending and it means 'to twist out of shape'. That's spot on. I'd like to warp Mrs Vomit Bagley, twisting and twisting, until her eyes pop and her arms and legs are wrapped right round her great big bum. That's another thing. Whenever I write the weeniest babiest little rude word Mrs V.B. goes bananas. I don't know what she'd do if I used *really* bad words like **** and **** and ****** (censored!!).

I looked up 'ramble' too. I liked what it said: 'To stroll about freely, as for relaxation, with no particular direction'. So that's *exactly* what I did today, instead of staying at boring old school. I bunked off and strolled round the town freely, as relaxed as anything. I had a little potter in Paperchase and bought this big

9

fat purple notebook with my pocket money. I'm going to write all my mega-manic ultra-scary stories in it, as warped and as rambly as I can make them. And I'll write *my* story too. I've written all about myself before in *The Story of Tracy Beaker*. So this can be *The Story of Tracy Beaker Two* or *Find Out What Happens Next to the Brave and Brilliant Tracy Beaker* or *Further Fabulous Adventures of the Tremendous Terrific Tracy Beaker* or *Read More About the Truly Terrible Tracy Beaker, Even More Wicked Than the Wicked Witch of the West.*

Yes. I was telling you about *The Wizard of Oz.* There's only one bit that I truly dread. I can't actually watch it. The first time I saw it I very nearly cried. (I *don't* cry, though. I'm tough. As old boots. New boots. The biggest fiercest reinforced Doc Martens . . .) It's the bit right at the end where Dorothy is getting fed up with being in Oz. Which is mad, if you ask me. Who'd want to go back to that boring black and white Kansas and be an ordinary kid where they take your dog away when you could dance round Oz in your ruby slippers? But Dorothy acts in an extremely dumb manner all the way through the film. You'd think she'd have sussed out for herself that all she had to do was click those ruby slippers and she'd get back home. That's it. That's the bit. Where she says, 'There's no place like home.'

It gets to me. Because there's no place like home for me. No place at all. I haven't got a home.

Well. I didn't have up until recently. Unless you count the Home. If a home has a capital letter at the front you can be pretty sure it isn't like a *real* home. It's just a dumping ground for kids with problems. The ugly kids, the bad kids, the daft kids. The ones no-one wants to foster. The kids way past their sell-by date so they're all chucked on the rubbish heap. There were certainly some ultra-rubbishy kids at that Home. Especially a certain Justine Littlewood . . .

We were Deadly Enemies once, but then we made up. I even gave Justine my special Mickey Mouse pen. I rather regretted

11

this actually and asked for it back the next day, pretending it had just been a loan, but Justine wasn't having any. There are no flies on Justine. No wasps, bees or any kind of bug.

It's weird, but I kind of miss Justine now. It was even fun when we were Deadly Enemies and we played the Dare Game. I've always been great at thinking up the silliest daftest rudest dares. I always dared everything and won until Justine came to the Children's Home. Then I *still* won. Most of the time. I *did*. But Justine could certainly invent some seriously wicked dares herself.

I miss her. I miss Louise too. And I especially miss Peter. This is even weirder. I couldn't stand weedy old Peter when he first came to the Home. But now it feels like he was my best ever friend. I wish I could see him. I especially wish I could see him right now. Because I'm all on my own and although it's great to be bunking off school and I've found the most brilliant hiding place in the whole world it is a little bit lonely.

I could do with a mate. When you're in care you need to make all the friends you can get because you don't have much family.

Well. I've got family.

I've got the loveliest prettiest best-ever mum in the whole world. She's this dead famous Hollywood movie star and she's in film after film, in so much demand that there isn't a minute of the day when she can see me so that's why I'm in care...

Who am I kidding??? Not you. Not even me. I used to carry on like that when I was little, and some kids took it all in and even acted like they were impressed. But now when I come out with all that movie guff they start to get this little curl of the lip and then the minute my back's turned I hear a splutter of laughter. And that's the *kinder* kids. The rest tell me straight to my face that I'm a nutter. They don't even believe my mum's an actress. I know for a fact she's been in *some* films. She sent me this big glossy photo of her in this negligée – but now kids nudge and giggle and say, 'What *kind* of film was your mum in, Tracy Beaker?'

13

So I duff them up. Sometimes literally. I'm very handy with my fists. Sometimes I just pretend it in my head. I should have pretended inside my head with Mrs Vomit Bagley. It isn't wise to tell teachers exactly what you think of them. She gave us this new piece of writing work this morning. About 'My Family'. It was supposed to be an exercise in autobiography. It's really a way for the teachers to be dead nosy and find out all sorts of secrets about the kids. Anyway, after she's told us all to start writing this 'My Family' stuff she squeezes her great hips in and out the desks till she gets to me. She leans over until her face is hovering a few inches from mine. I thought for one seriously scary second she was going to *kiss* me!

'Of course, *you* write about your foster mother, Tracy,' she whispers, her Tic-Tac minty breath tickling my ear.

She thought she was whispering discreetly, but every single kid in the room looked up and stared. So I stared straight back and edged as far away from Mrs V.B. as I could and said firmly, 'I'm going to write about my *real* mother, Mrs Bagley.'

So I did. Page after page. My writing got a bit sprawly and I gave up on spelling and stopped bothering about full stops and capital letters because they're such a waste of time, but I wrote this *amazing* account of me and my mum. Only I never finished it. Because Mrs V.B. does another Grand Tour of the class, bending over and reading your work over your shoulder in the most off-putting way possible, and she gets to me and leans over, and then she sniffs inwards and sighs. I thought she was just going to have the usual old nag about Neatness and Spelling and Punctuation – but this time she was miffed about the content, not the presentation.

'You and your extraordinary imagination, Tracy,' she said, in this falsely sweet patronizing tone. She even went 'Tut tut', shaking her head, still with this silly smirk on her face.

'What do you mean?' I said, sharpish.

'Tracy! Don't take that rude tone with me, dear.' There was an edge to her voice and all. 'I did my best to explain about Autobiography. It means you tell a *true* story about yourself and your own life.'

'It *is* true. All of it,' I said indignantly.

'Really, Tracy!' she said, and she started reading bits out, not trying to keep her voice down now, revving up for public proclamation.

' "My mum is starring in a Hollywood movie with George Clooney and Tom Cruise and Brad Pitt and they all think she's wonderful and want to be her boyfriend. Her new movie is going to star Leonardo DiCaprio as her younger brother and she's got really matey with Leonardo at rehearsals and he's seen the photo of me she carries around in her wallet and he says I look real cute and wants to write to me," ' Mrs V.B. read out in this poisonous high-pitched imitation of my voice.

The entire class collapsed. Some of the kids practically wet themselves laughing. Mrs V.B. had this smirk puckering her lips. 'Do you really believe this, Tracy?' she asked.

So I said, 'I really believe that you're a stupid hideous old bag who could only get a part in a movie about bloodsucking vampire bats.'

I thought for a moment she was going to prove her bat-star qualities by flying at my neck and biting me with her fangs. She certainly wanted to. But she just marched me out of the room instead and told me to stand outside the door because she was sick of my insolence.

I said she made *me* sick and it was a happy chance that her name was Mrs V. Bagley. The other kids might wonder whether the V. stood for Vera or Violet or Vanessa, but I was certain her first name was Vomit, and dead appropriate too, given her last name, because she looked like the contents of a used vomit bag.

She went back into the classroom when I was only halfway through so I said it to myself, slumping against the wall and staring at my shoes. I said I was Thrilled to Bits to miss out on her lesson because she was boring boring boring and couldn't teach for toffee. She couldn't teach for fudge, nougat, licorice or Turkish delight. I declared I was utterly Ecstatic to be Outside.

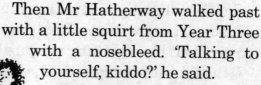

Then Mr Hatherway walked past with a little squirt from Year Three with a nosebleed. 'Talking to yourself, kiddo?' he said.

'No, I'm talking to my shoes,' I said crossly.

I expected him to have a go at me too but he just nodded and mopped the little spurting scarlet fountain. 'I have a quiet chat to *my* shoes when things are getting me down,' he said. 'Very understanding friends, shoes. I find my old Hush Puppies especially comforting.'

The little squirt gave a whimper and Mr Hatherway gave him another mop. 'Come on, pal, we'd better get you some first aid.'

He gave me a little nod and they walked on. Up until that moment I was convinced that this new school was 100% horrible. Now it was maybe 1% OK, because I quite liked Mr Hatherway. Not that I had any chance of having him as my teacher, not unless I was shoved out of Year Six right to the bottom of the Juniors. And the school was still 99% the pits, so I decided to clear off out of it.

It was easy-peasy. I waited till playtime

18

when Mrs V.B. waved me away, her nostrils pinched like I smelled bad. So I returned the compliment and held my own nose but she pretended not to notice. It was music in the hall with Miss Smith after playtime so I was someone else's responsibility then. Only I wasn't going to stick around for music because Miss Smith keeps picking on me too, just because of that one time I experimented with alternative uses of a drumstick. So I moseyed down the corridor like I was going to the toilets only I went right on walking, round the corner, extra sharpish past Reception (though Mrs Ludovic was busy mopping the little kid with the nosebleed. It looked like World War Three in her office) and then quick out the door and off across the yard. The main gate was locked but that presented no problem at all for SuperTracy. I was up that wall and over in a flash. I did fall over the other side and both my knees got a bit chewed up but that didn't bother me.

They hurt quite a lot now, even though they've stopped bleeding. They both look pretty dirty. I've probably introduced all sorts of dangerous germs into my bloodstream and any minute now I'll develop a high fever and start frothing at the mouth. I don't feel very well actually. And I'm *starving*. I wish I hadn't spent all my money on this notebook. I especially wish I hadn't picked one the exact purple of a giant bar of Cadbury's milk chocolate. I shall start slavering all over it soon.

I'd really like to call it a day and push off back to Cam's but the clock's just struck and it's only one o'clock. Lunchtime. Only I haven't any lunch. I can't go back till teatime or Cam will get suspicious. I *could* show her my savaged knees and say I had a Dire Accident and got sent home, but Cam would think I'd been fighting again. I got in enough trouble the last time. It wasn't *fair*. I didn't start the fight.

It was all that Roxanne Green's fault. She made this sneery remark to her friends about my T-shirt. She was showing off in her new DKNY T-shirt, zigzagging her shoulders this way and that, so I started imitating her and everyone laughed. So she goes, 'What label is *your* T-shirt, Tracy?'

Before I could make anything up she says, '*I* know. It's Oxfam!'

Everyone laughed again but this time it was awful so I got mad and called Roxanne various names and then she called *me* names and most of it was baby stuff but then she said the B word – and added that it was true in my case because I really didn't have a dad.

So I had to smack her one then, didn't I? It was only fair. Only Roxanne and all her little girly hangers-on didn't think it was fair and they told Mrs Vomit Bagley and she *certainly* didn't think it was fair and she told Mr Donne the headteacher and, guess what, he didn't think it was fair either. He rang Cam and asked her to come to the school for a Quiet Word. I was yanked along to the study too and I said lots of words not at *all* quietly, but Cam put her arm round me and hissed in my ear, 'Cool it, Trace.'

I tried. I thought c-o-o-l and imagined a beautiful blue lake of water and me swimming slowly along – but I was so sizzling mad the water started to bubble all around me and I ended up boiling over and telling the head what I thought of him and his poxy teachers and putrid pupils. (Get my vocabulary, Mrs V.B.!)

I very nearly ended up being excluded. Which is mad. I should have been even cheekier because I don't *want* to go to this terrible old school.

So I've excluded myself.

I'm here.

In my own secret place. Dead exclusive. My very own house.

Home!

Well, it's not exactly *homely* at the moment. It needs a good going over with a vacuum or two. Or three or four or five. And even though it's kind of empty it needs a spot of tidying. There are empty beer cans and McDonald's cartons chucked all over the place, and all kinds of freebie papers and advertising bumpf litter the hall so you're wading ankle-deep when you come in the front door. Only I didn't, seeing as it's locked and bolted and boarded over. I came in the back, through the broken window, ever so carefully.

I went in the back garden because I was mooching round and round the streets, dying for a wee. I came across this obviously empty house down at the end of a little cul-de-sac with big brambles all over the place giving lots of cover so I thought I'd nip over the wall quick and relieve myself. Which I did, though a black cat suddenly streaked past, which made me jump and lose concentration so I very nearly weed all over my trainers.

When I was relieved and decent I tried to catch the cat, pretending this was a jungle and the cat was a tiger and I was all set to train it but the cat went 'Purr-lease!' and stalked off with its tail in the air.

I explored the jungle by myself and spotted the broken window and decided to give the house a recce too.

It's a great house. It hasn't quite got all mod cons any more. The water's been turned off and the lights won't switch on and the radiators are cold. But there's still a sofa in the living room, quite a swish one, red velvet. Some plonker's put his muddy boots all over it, but I've been scratching at it with my fingernails and I think it'll clean up a treat.

I could bring a cushion. And a blanket. And some *food*. Yeah.

Next time.

But now it's time for me to go . . . back to Cam.

Cam's Home

Cam is fostering me. It was all my idea. When I was back in the Children's Home I was pretty desperate to be fostered. *Ugly* desperate. They'd even tried advertising me in the papers, this gungy little description of me outlining all my bad points together with a school photo where I was scowling – and so no-one came forward, which didn't exactly surprise me. Though it was still awful. Especially when one of the kids at school brought the newspaper into school and showed everyone. That was a different school. It wasn't much cop either. But it was marginally better than this one. This one is the worst ever.

It's Cam's fault. She said I had to go there. Because it's the nearest one. I *knew* I'd hate it from the very first day. It's an old school, all red brick and brown paint and smelly cloakrooms and nearly all the teachers are old too. They sound like they've all been to this old-fashioned elocution school to get that horrid sarcastic tone to their voices.

You know: 'Oh, that's really *clever* of you, Tracy Beaker' when you spill 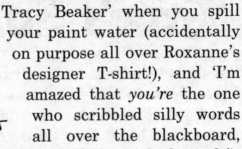 your paint water (accidentally on purpose all over Roxanne's designer T-shirt!), and 'I'm amazed that *you're* the one who scribbled silly words all over the blackboard, Tracy Beaker' (wonderfully wicked words!), and 'Can you possibly speak up a bit, Tracy Beaker, I think there's a deaf old lady at the other end of the street who didn't quite catch that' (I *had* to raise my voice because how else can I get the other kids in my group to listen to me?).

I hate it when we have to split up for group work. They all fit into these neat little groups: Roxanne and her gang, Almost-Alan-Shearer and the football crazies, Basher Dixon and his henchmen, Wimpy Lizzie and Dopey Dawn and that lot, Brainbox Hannah and Swotty Andrew – they're all divided up. And then there's me.

Mrs V.B. puts me in different groups each time. Sometimes I'm in a group all by myself. I don't care. I prefer it. I hate them all.

Cam says I should try to make friends. I don't *want* to be friends with that seriously sad bunch of losers. I keep moaning to Cam that it's a rubbish school and telling her to send me somewhere else. She's useless. Well, she did try going down to the Guildhall and seeing if they could swop me somewhere else but they said the other schools in the area are oversubscribed.

She just accepted it. Didn't make any kind of fuss. If you want anything in this world you've got to fight for it. I should know.

'You're on their waiting list,' Cam said, as if she thought I'd be pleased.

What use is that? I've been waiting half my life to *get* a life. I thought my big chance had come when Cam came to the Children's Home to research this boring old article about kids in care. (She only got £100 for it and I was barely mentioned!) I thought she might do as a foster mum as she's a writer and so am I.

She needed quite a lot of persuading.

But I can be pretty determined when I want. And I *did* want Cam. Badly.

So when she said, 'Right then, Tracy, let's give it a go. You and me. OK?' it was more than OK. I was over the moon. Soaring straight up into the solar system. I couldn't wait to get out of the Children's Home. I got dead impatient with Elaine the Pain my social worker because she seemed to be trying to slow things down instead of speed them up.

'No point in rushing things, Tracy,' she said.

I felt there was *every* point. I didn't want Cam to change her mind. She was having to go to all these interviews and meetings and courses and she's not really that sort of person. She doesn't like to be bossed around and told what to do. Like me. I was scared she might start to think it was all too much hassle.

But *eventually* we had a weekend together and that was great. Cam wanted it to be a very laid-back weekend – a walk in the park, a video or two, and a takeaway pizza. I said I did all that sort of stuff already at the Children's Home and couldn't we do something special to celebrate our first weekend together?

I told you I can be pretty persuasive. Cam took me to Chessington World of Adventures and it was truly great and she even bought me this huge python with beady green eyes and a black forked tongue. She dithered long and hard about it, saying she didn't want it to look like she was buying my affection, but I made the python wind round and round her beguilingly. He 'told' her he was desperate to be bought because the shopkeeper was really mean to him just because he'd got a teeny bit peckish and gobbled up a furry bunny and several toy mice as a little snack.

Cam bought him though she said she was mad and that she'd be eating bread and cheese for the rest of the week as the entry tickets and burger and chips for lunch had already cost a fortune.

I should have realized she can be a boring old meanie when it comes to money but I wanted Cam to foster me so much that I didn't focus on her bad points.

Maybe she didn't focus on *my* bad points???

Anyway, it was like we were both wearing our rose-coloured glasses and we smiled in our pink-as-petals perfect world and on Sunday evening when I had to go back to the Home Cam hugged me almost as tight as I hugged her and promised that she really wanted to go through with things and foster me.

So she did. And that's really where my story should have ended. Happily Ever After. Only I'm not always happy. And actually I'm not even sure Cam is either.

It was fine at first. Elaine says we went through this Honeymoon Period. Is it any wonder I call her a pain? She comes out with such yucky expressions. But I suppose Cam and I were a little bit like newly weds. We went everywhere together, sometimes even hand-in-hand, and whenever I wanted anything I could generally persuade her and I was careful not to get too stroppy because I didn't want her to go off me and send me back. But after a bit . . .

I don't know. Somehow it all changed. Cam wouldn't always take me out for treats and buy me stuff. Stuff I seriously *need*, like designer clothes, else I get picked on by poisonous girls like Roxanne. Cam says she can't afford it – which can't be true. I know for a fact she gets paid a fortune by the authorities for looking after me. It's a bit of a rip-off, if you ask me. And this is all on top of what she earns from being a writer.

Cam says she doesn't earn much as a writer. Peanuts, she says. Well, that's her fault. She doesn't write the right stuff. She's wasting her time writing these yawny articles for big boring papers that haven't got proper pictures. And her books are even worse. They're dreary paperbacks about poor women with problems. I mean, who wants to read that sort of rubbish? I wish she'd write more romantic stuff. I keep telling Cam she wants to get cracking on those great glossy books everyone reads on their holidays. Where all the women are beautiful with heaps of different designer outfits and all the men have

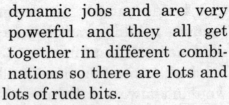

dynamic jobs and are very powerful and they all get together in different combinations so there are lots and lots of rude bits.

Cam just laughs at me and says she can't stick those sort of books. She says she doesn't mind not being a successful writer.

I mind. I want a foster mum I can show off about. I can't show off about Cam because no-one's ever heard of her. And she's not pretty or sexy or glamorous. She doesn't wear any make-up and her hair's too short to style so it just sticks straight up and her clothes are *awful* – T-shirts and jeans all the time and they're certainly *not* designer.

Her home is just as shabby too. I hoped I'd get to live in a big house with swish furniture and lots of fancy ornaments, but Cam lives in this poky little flat. She hasn't even got any proper *carpet*, she's just polished up the bare floorboards and has a few rugs scattered about. Quite good fun if I fancy a slide but they look hopeless. You should see her sofa too! It's leather but it's all cracked so she has to hide it with this old patchwork quilt and some lumpy tapestry cushions she cross-stitched herself. She tried to show me how to do cross-stitch. No wonder that's what it's called. The more I stitched the crosser I got, and I soon gave up in disgust.

I've got my own bedroom but it's not a patch on my room at the Children's Home. It's not much bigger than a *cupboard*. Cam's so mean too. She said I could choose to have my bedroom exactly the way I wanted. Well, I had some great ideas. I wanted a king-size bed with a white satin duvet and my own dressing

table with lights all round the mirror like a film star and white carpet as soft and thick as cat fur and my own computer to write my stories on and my own sound system and a giant white television and video and a trapeze hanging from the ceiling so I could practise circus tricks and my own ensuite bathroom so I could splash all day in my own private bubble bath.

Cam acted like I was *joking*. When she realized I wasn't joining in the general laughter she said, 'Come *on*, Trace, how could all that stuff ever fit in the box room?'

Yeah, quite. Why should I be stuck in the box room? Am I a box? Why can't I have Cam's room? I mean, she's got hardly any stuff, just a lot of books and a little bed. She could easily fit in the box room.

I did my best to persuade her. I wheedled and whined for all I was worth – but she didn't budge. So I ended up in this little rubbish room and I'm supposed to think it a huge big deal because I was allowed to choose the colour paint and pick a new duvet cover and curtains. I chose black to match my mood.

I didn't think Cam would take me seriously but she gave in on that one. Black walls. Black ceiling. She suggested luminous silver stars which are kind of a good idea. I'm not too keen on the dark. I'm not *scared*. I'm not scared of anything. But I like to look up from

34

my bed and see those stars glowing up above.

Cam hunted around and found some black sheets with silver stars and made curtains to match. She's pretty useless at sewing and the hems go up and down a bit but I suppose she was trying her best. She calls my black room the 'bat cave'. She's bought me several little black velvet toy bats to hang from the ceiling. They're quite cute really. And my python lies on the floor by the door and acts like a draught excluder and attacks anyone who dares try to barge in on us.

Like Jane and Liz. I can't stand Jane and Liz. They are Cam's friends. They keep coming over and sticking their noses in. I thought they were

OK at first. Jane is big (you should see the size of her bum!) and Liz is little and bouncy. Jane took me swimming once (she's not a pretty sight in her swimming costume) and it was quite good fun actually. There was a chute into the water and a wave machine and Jane let me ride on her shoulders and didn't get huffy when I pretended she was a whale. She even spouted water for me. But then she came over one day when Cam and I were having this little dispute – well, kind of mega-argument when I was letting rip yelling all sorts of stuff – and later when I was sulking in my bat cave I heard Jane telling Cam that she was daft to put up with all my nonsense and she knew I had had a hard time but that didn't give me licence to be such a Royal Pain in the Bottom. (A pain wouldn't have a chance attacking *her* bottom.)

I still thought Liz was OK. I was worried at first because she's a teacher but she's not a *bit* like Mrs V.B. She knows all these really rude jokes and she can be a great laugh. She's got her own rollerblades and she let me borrow them which was great. *I* was great too. I simply whizzed around and didn't fall over once and looked seriously cool – but then when I started getting on to Cam that it was time she bought me my *own* rollerblades seeing I was so super-skilled Liz got a bit edgy and told me that Cam wasn't made of money.

I wish!

Then Liz started off this boring old lecture about Caring not being the same as Spending Money and it was almost as if she'd morphed into Mrs Vomit Bagley before my very eyes!

I still thought Liz was kind of cool though but then one evening she came round late when I was in bed in the Bat Cave and I think maybe Cam was crying in the living room because we'd had some boring old set-to about something . . . I forget what. Well, I *don't* forget, I happened to have borrowed a tenner out of her purse – I didn't *steal* it – and anyway if she's my foster mum now she *should* fork out for me, and she's so mean she doesn't give me enough pocket money, and it was only a measly ten-pound note – I could have nicked a twenty – and why did she leave her purse lying around if she gets so fussed about cash going missing? – she's not part of the real

world, old Cam, she wouldn't have lasted five
minutes in the Children's Home.

Anyway, Liz came round and I
slithered round my door like my
python so I could hear what they
were saying. I figured it would be
about me. And it was.

Liz kept asking Cam what this
latest crisis was all about and Cam
kept quiet for a bit but then out it
all came: naughty little Tracy is
a thief. Cam started on about some other stuff
too. OK, I borrowed one of her pens – well,
several – and some silly old locket that her
mum had given her. I didn't mean to buckle
it. I was only trying to prise it open to see
what she had inside.

I felt Cam was being a mean old tell-tale –
and Liz was encouraging her for all she was
worth, saying it was good for her to let it all
out and have a moan and howl. Liz came out
with all this s-t-u-p-i-d stuff that I was just
nicking for affection and attention. All these
teachers and social workers have got their
heads full of this rubbish. I nicked the stuff
because I was short of cash and needed a pen
and . . . well, I just wanted the locket. I

38

thought I could maybe put a picture of my mum in it. My real mum. I've got a photo, and she's looking dead glamorous, a true movie star, smiling and smiling. Guess what she's smiling at! This little baby in her arms  tugging at her gorgeous long blonde hair. It's me!

I wish Cam had long hair. I wish she looked glamorous. I wish she was something special like a film star. I wish she smiled more. She just slumps round all draggy and depressed. Over me.

She had a good cry to Liz and said she was useless and that it wasn't working out the way she'd hoped.

I *knew* it. I *knew* she wouldn't want me. Well. See if I care.

Liz said that this was just a stage, and that I was acting out and testing my limits.

'She's testing *my* limits, I tell you,' said Cam.

'You mustn't let her get to you so,' said Liz. 'Lighten up a bit, Cam. Don't let your life revolve around Tracy all the time. You don't

39

ever go out any more. You've even given up your classes.'

'Yes, well, I can't leave Tracy in the evening. I did bring up the idea of a babysitter but she was insulted.'

'What about your morning swimming then? You were getting really fit. Why don't you take Tracy too, before school? Jane says she loved it at the baths.'

'There just isn't time. We have enough hassle getting her ready for school at nine. And, oh God, that's another thing. She isn't settling and the head keeps ringing me up and I don't know what to do about it.'

'How about telling Tracy how you feel?'

'Tracy's not bothered about the way *I* feel. It's the way *she* feels that matters. And she's not feeling too great either at the moment. So she takes it out on me.'

'Try standing up to her for once. Put her in her place,' says horrible old Liz.

'That's just it. That's why she's so difficult. She doesn't know her place because she hasn't ever had one. A place of her own,' says Cam.

It made me feel good that she could suss that out and bad because I don't want her to pity me. I don't want her to foster me because she feels sorry for me. I want her to foster me because she's dead lonely and it gives her life a purpose and she's crazy about me. She says she cares about me but she doesn't love me like a real mum. She doesn't want to buy me treats every single day and give me loads of money and keep me home from school because it's so horrible.

I'm not *ever* going back. I can bunk off every day, easy-peasy. I timed it to perfection, arriving back at Cam's dead on time. She was sitting on her squashy old sofa writing her sad old story in her notebook. I made her jump when I came barging in but she smiled. I suddenly felt weird, like I'd been missing her or something, so I ran over to her and bounced down beside her.

'Hey, Trace, watch the sofa!' she said, struggling back into the upright position. 'You'll break it. You'll break me!'

'Half the springs are broken already.'

'Look, I never pretended this was House Beautiful.'

'Hovel Hideous, more like,' I said, getting up and roaming round the shabby furniture, giving it a kick.

'Don't do that, Tracy,' Cam said sharply.

Aha! It was standing-up-to-Tracy time! Well, I can stand up to her. And walk all over her too.

Cam saw me squaring up and wilted. 'Don't start, Tracy. I've had a hard day. You know that article I wrote?'

'Rejected?'

'So I'm *de*jected. And I'm stuck halfway through Chapter Four of my novel and—'

'And you want to write something that will *sell*. Something action-packed!' I pretended to karate chop her. I didn't touch her but I made her blink. 'Lively!' I jumped up and down in front of her. 'And sexy!' I waggled my hips and batted my eyelashes.

'Yeah yeah yeah,' said Cam.

'I'm going to make my fortune as a writer, you wait and see,' I said. I looked at the little bits Cam had scribbled in her notebook. 'I can write heaps more than that. I wrote pages and pages and pages today, practically a whole book.'

'Was that for English?'

'No, it was . . .' Oh-oh. Caution required. 'It was just something private I'm writing. At playtime and in the lunch hour.'

'Can I have a look?'

'No!' I don't want her to see this purple notebook. I keep it hidden in my school bag. Otherwise she might wonder when I bought it. And where I got the cash. She might start going through her purse again and we don't want another one of *those* rows.

'OK, OK, it's private, right. But couldn't I have one little peep?'

'You're getting as bad as old Vomit Bagley. She made us do this Exercise in Autobiography, the nosy old bag, all this stuff about "My Family".'

Cam stiffened and forgot about my private writing – as I intended!

'She says to me that I should write about my *foster* mum—'

'And did you?'

'No, I wrote about my mum. And how she's an actress in Hollywood and so busy she can't come and see me. You know.'

'Yeah. I know.'

'Only old Vomit Bag didn't believe me. She made fun of me.'

'That's horrible!'

'You believe me, don't you, Cam? About my mum?' I watched her very carefully.

'Well . . . I know just how much your mum means to you, Tracy.'

'Ha! You think it's all rubbish, don't you? A story I made up.'

'No! Not if . . . if you think it's true.'

'Well, it's not true.' I suddenly shouted it. 'None of it's true. I made it all up. It's dead babyish and pathetic. She's not an actress at all. She just can't be bothered to get in touch.'

'You don't know that, Tracy.' Cam tried to put her arm round me but I jerked free.

'I *do* know. I haven't seen her for *years*. I used to wait and wait and wait for her in the Children's Home. I must have been mad. She isn't ever going to come and get me. If someone said, "Do you remember anyone called Tracy Beaker?" she'd probably look vague and go, "Hang on – Tracy? Sounds familiar. Who *is* she, exactly?" Fat lot she cares. Well, I don't care either. I don't *want* her for my mum.'

I didn't know I was going to say all that. Cam

was staring at me. I stared back at
My throat felt dry and my eyes prickled. I very
nearly started crying, only of course I don't
ever cry.

Cam was looking at
me. My eyes blurred so
that she went all
fuzzy. I took a step
forward, holding
out my hands like I
was feeling my way
through fog.
Then the phone
rang. We both jumped. I blinked. Cam said to
leave it. But I can't stand leaving a phone
ringing, so I answered it.

It was Elaine the Pain. She didn't want to
talk to me. She wanted to speak to Cam.
Typical. She's *my* social worker. And it was
about *me*. But she had to tell Cam first. And
then she told me.

You'll never ever ever guess.

It's my mum.

She's been in touch.

She wants to see me!

Elaine's Home

I haven't been to Elaine's *home* home. Just her office. She's done her best to turn it *into* a home. She's got all these photos of kids on the wall. I'm there somewhere. She's used the photo where I'm crossing my eyes and sticking out my tongue. She's got a similarly cross-eyed giant bear prowling the top of her filing cabinet, terrorizing a little droopy-eared mauve rabbit. There's an old Valentine propped on her desk which says inside (I had a quick nose), 'To my Little Bunny from Big Bear'. Y-U-C-K! She has a framed photo of this ultra-weedy guy with thick glasses who must be Big Bear. There are several framed mottoes too, like: 'You don't have to be mad to work here but it helps' and a poem about an old woman wearing purple and some long drivelly meditation about Listening to Your Inner Child.

Never mind Elaine's Inner Child. I am her Outer Child and it's mega-difficult to make contact with her, even when I bawl my head off.

'Now calm down, Tracy,' she said.

'I don't want to calm down!' I yelled. 'I want  to see my mum. I've waited long enough. Like, *years*! So I want to see my mum NOW!'

'You don't get anywhere by yelling, Tracy,' said Elaine. 'You should know how things work by now.'

'I know how they *don't* work! *Why* can't I see my mum right this minute?'

'Because we need to prepare for this meeting.'

'Prepare! I've been waiting half my life! I couldn't get more prepared if I tried.'

'That's just it, Tracy. We don't want you to get too worked up about things.'

'So you think telling me my mum wants to see me and *then* telling me I can't see her is going to calm me *down*????'

'I didn't say you can't see her. Of course you can see her.'

'When?'

'When we can all arrange an appropriate date.'

'Who's this "we"?'

'Well. I shall need to be there. And Cam.'

'Why? Why can't it just be my mum and me?'

It was just my mum and me once. I can remember it. I *can*. We had a great time, my mum and me. She's incredibly beautiful, my mum. Lovely long curly fair hair all round her shoulders, dead smart, with high heels. She looks amazing. Well, she did. Last time I saw her. Quite a while ago.

A long long time ago.

I *do* remember that last time. I was in the Home then but Mum visited me at first – she even gave me this doll, and she took me to McDonald's. It was a great day out. And she kissed me goodbye. I remember the way her blonde curls tickled my cheek and the sweet powdery way she smelled. I clung on tight round her neck, so tight that when she straightened up I was still clinging to her like a monkey, and that annoyed her because I got my muddy shoes over her smart black skirt and I was scared she was cross and wouldn't come back.

I said, 'You *will* come back, Mum, won't you? Next Saturday? You'll take me to McDonald's again? Promise?'

She promised.

But she didn't come back. I waited that Saturday. The Saturday after that. Saturday after Saturday after Saturday.

She didn't come back. She didn't come because she got this amazing offer from Hollywood and she starred in this incredible movie and—

And who am I kidding? Why am I spouting the same old babyish rubbish? She probably wasn't ever a proper actress. She certainly hasn't been in any Hollywood movies that I know of. She didn't come back because she couldn't be bothered. She left me in care. For years.

I was taken into care because she didn't look after me properly. She kept going off with this boyfriend and leaving me. And then she got this new scary guy who whacked me one whenever I yelled. I've had a little peep in my files. Though I can remember some of it too. Stuff that still gives me nightmares.

So why do I want to see my mum so much?

I don't want to see her.

I do.

Even after the way she's treated me?

She's still my mum.

I've got Cam now.

She's not my mum, she's just a foster parent. And she's sick of me anyway.

Is she?

I don't know.

I suppose I need to talk it over with Elaine.

So the next time I see her I'm all set. She's all smiles.

'Ah, Tracy, you'll be pleased to know it's all fixed now, this special meeting with your mum.' She beams at me, as happy as a bunny in a field of lettuce.

'I don't want to see her now,' I said.

Elaine's bunny nose went twitch-twitch-twitch. 'What?'

'You heard. I don't have to see her, not if I don't want. And I *don't* want.'

'Tracy, you are going to be the death of me,' she said, blowing upwards over her big bunny teeth. Then her eyes crossed a little with concentration and I knew she was counting up to ten, s-l-o-w-l-y. It's her little way of dealing with me. When she got to ten she gave me this big false smile. 'I understand, Tracy,' she said.

'No you don't.'

'It's only natural you feel anxious about this meeting. It obviously means a great deal to you. And you don't want to risk getting let down. But I've had several phone conversations with your mother and she seems as keen as you to meet. I'm sure she'll turn up this time, Tracy.'

'I *said*, I don't want to see her,' I declared, but I knew I wasn't kidding her.

She tried to kid me though. 'OK, Tracy, you don't want to see your mum – so I'll phone up right this minute and cancel everything,' she said, and she started dialling.

'Hey, hang about. No need to be quite so hasty,' I said.

Elaine giggled. 'Got you!'

'I don't think that's very professional of you, teasing like that,' I said, dead haughty.

'You would try the patience of a professional saint, Tracy,' said Elaine, and she ruffled my hair. 'Now, how are things with you and Cam?'

'OK. I suppose.'

'She's one hundred and one per cent supporting you over seeing your mum, you know, but it must be a little bit hard for her.'

'Well. That's what being a foster mum is all about, isn't it? Taking a back seat when necessary. Encouraging all contact with natural families. I've read the leaflets.'

'You're all heart, Tracy,' said Elaine, sighing.

'Not me, Elaine. Totally heart*less*,' I said.

So . . . I'm seeing my mum tomorrow! Which is maybe why I'm wide awake now at three o'clock in the morning. Scribbling away. And wondering what she'll be like. And if she'll really come.

Oh-oh. Stirrings from next door. Cam's spotted my light.

Later. I thought she might be a bit narked. But she made us both a cup of tea and then we sat at either end of my bed, sipping away. I don't usually like her ropy old herbal tea but she'd bought a special strawberry packet that doesn't taste too horrible.

I thought she might want a heart-to-heart
(even though I haven't got one) but thank
goodness she just started talking about this
story she used to make up when she was a
little kid and couldn't sleep. I said, 'Yeah, I do
that, really scary bloodthirsty ghost stories,'
and she said, 'No, little ghoul, this was
supposed to be a *comfort* story,' and she
started on about pretending her duvet was a
big white bird and she'd be flying on its back
in the starlight and then it would take her to
a lake and they'd float on it in the dark and
then they'd go to its great mossy nest . . .

'All slime and bird's muck, right?'

'Wrong! All soft and fresh and downy, and
the big white bird would spread its wings
and I'd huddle underneath in the quiet and

the warmth, hearing its heart beat under its snowy feathers.'

'Oh, I get it. This is the Get-you-back-to-sleep story,' I said – but after she'd taken my cup and tucked me up and ruffled my curls (why do they all do that, like I'm some unruly little puppy?) and I was left in the dark I tried out the story myself. Only I was in my black bat cave, and I'm Tracy Beaker, not a silly old softie like Cam, so I made up this big black vampire bat and we swooped through the night together. We'd zap straight through certain windows and nip Mrs V.B. in the neck or nibble Roxanne right on the end of her nose and flap out again the second they started screaming. I think it took me to its real big black bat cave to hang by our toes with all our brother bats only I might have been asleep by then.

I'm awake now. Early. Waiting.

I wonder if she'll turn up?

She did, she did, she did!!!

Cam came with me to Elaine's. But she waited outside and, surprise surprise, Elaine did too. So the mega-meet of the century took place in private. Just me and my mum.

I was sitting in Elaine's room, swivelling round and round in her little chair on wheels, when this woman comes straight in and stands there blinking at me. A small woman with very bright blonde hair and a lot of lipstick, wearing a very short skirt and very high heels.

A beautiful woman with long fair hair and a lovely face in the most stylish sexy clothes.

My mum.

I knew her straight away.

She didn't know me. She went on blinking, like she'd just poked her mascara wand in her eye. 'Tracy?' she said, looking round, as if the room was full of kids.

'Hi,' I said, in this silly little squeak.

'You're not my Tracy!' said mum, shaking her head at me. 'You're too big!'

I'm quite small and skinny for my age so I

didn't get what she was on about.

'My Tracy's just a little kid. A funny little kid with weird sticky-out plaits. The tantrums when it was hair-brushing time!' She peered at me. 'Was that really you?'

I held out a strand of hair and mimed plaiting it.

'You had a filthy temper when you were a toddler,' said Mum. 'It *is* you, isn't it? My Tracy!'

'Mum.'

'Well!'

There was a bit of a pause. Mum half held her arms out but then changed her mind, acting like she was just stretching.

'Well,' she said again. 'How have you been then, darling? Did you miss me, eh?'

I did a rapid rewind through the years, remembering. I wanted to tell her what it was like. But I couldn't seem to get my act together at all. I'm the lippiest gabbiest kid ever, ask anyone – but now all I could do was nod.

Mum looked a bit disappointed by my response. '*I've* been driven crazy thinking about you!' she said. 'I kept making all these plans to get you back, but things kept going haywire. I was tied up with this and that . . .'

'Films?' I whispered.

'Mmm.'

'In Hollywood?'

'Not exactly.'

'But you *are* an actress, aren't you, Mum?'

'Yes, sweetie. And I do a lot of modelling too. All sorts. Anyway. I always planned for you and me to get back together, like I said. But I wanted it to be perfect, see.'

I didn't see. But I didn't say.

'I kept getting mixed up with the wrong kind of guy,' Mum confided, perching on the edge of Elaine's desk and rootling in her handbag.

'I remember,' I said cautiously. 'There was one . . . I hated him.'

'Yeah, well, like I said, there have been a few. And my latest! A total pig!' She shook her head and lit a cigarette, taking a long drag.

Elaine has a strict non-smoking policy in her room. In the whole building. If any of the staff or the clients want a quick fag they have to huddle outside the back entrance. I was sure the smoke alarm was going to go off any second.

'Mum,' I said, nodding at the crossed-out cigarette sign prominently displayed on the wall.

Mum tutted contemptuously and took another puff. 'I gave my heart to that man,' she said, tapping herself on her chest and scattering ash down her jumper. 'Do you know what he did with it?' She leant towards me. '*Stamped* on it!' Her high heel jerked as if she was doing the stamping.

'Men!' I said sympathetically, in the tone Cam and Liz and Jane frequently used.

Mum looked at me and then burst into peals of laughter. I felt daft and swivelled round and round on Elaine's chair.

'Hey, don't do that, you're making me feel giddy. Come here! Haven't you got a kiss for your mum after all this time?'

'Sure,' I said shyly, though I'm not really the kissy-kissy type.

Mum bent down, her head on one side. I pecked at her powdery cheek – and then the sweet smell of her made me suddenly clutch her tight.

'Hey, hey, careful, sweetie! Watch my cigarette! No need

to be so dramatic. Looks like *you're* the little actress!' She dabbed at my face. 'Real tears!'

'No they're not,' I said, sniffling. 'I don't ever cry. It's hayfever.'

'Where's the hay?' said Mum, peering round Elaine's office. Her ash was building up again. She tapped it into Elaine's special Bunnikins mug. I hoped Elaine would look inside before making herself a cup of coffee.

'I get allergic to all sorts,' I said, wiping my nose.

'Hey, hey, haven't you got a tissue?' said Mum, tutting at me. 'I hope you're not allergic to *me*.'

'Maybe it's your perfume – though it smells lovely.'

'Ah,' said Mum, dabbing at me with her own tissue. 'That's my Poison. That pig forked out for a huge bottle just before he cleared off. I'd like to poison him all right! The nerve! Left me for some silly little kid barely older than you.'

'Typical!' I said.

Mum chuckled again. 'Where do you get all your quaint ways, eh?'

'Cam says "typical" a lot,' I said, without really thinking.

'Who's Cam?' said Mum.

I felt a little *thunk* in my stomach. 'My . . . my foster mum.'

Mum straightened up and threw the damp tissue into Elaine's wastebin. Well, she missed, but she didn't seem to care. 'Ah!' she said, pinching the end of her cigarette so that she squeezed the light out of it. She threw it in the direction of the wastebin, missing again. 'She's the one who's taken a fancy to you. Your social worker –' Mum lowered her voice slightly, gesturing round the office – 'what's her name?'

'Elaine. The pain.'

Mum stopped looking stroppy and giggled again. 'She is, isn't she! Still, you watch your lip, Tracy.'

I stuck my lip right out and crossed my eyes, like I was watching it.

Mum sighed and shook her head at me. 'Cheeky! Anyway, she gets in touch with me – eventually – and tells me this woman has bobbed up out of the blue and has taken you out of the Children's Home. Right?'

I nodded.

Mum lit up another fag, getting dead irritated now. 'Why did you go along with it? You don't want to live with this woman, do you?'

I didn't know what to do. I just kind of shrugged my shoulders.

'She sounds a bit suspect, if you ask me. Single woman, no spare cash – obviously scruffy standards, judging by your little outfit. Where did she get your clothes, a jumble sale?'

'You got it.'

'No! You'd think they'd be a bit more picky with their foster parents. Couldn't they have found anyone better? Anyway, you don't need a foster mum. It's not like you're an orphan. You've *got* a mum. Me.'

I blinked at her.

She sighed again, dragging on her cigarette. 'I wanted you safe and sound in the Children's Home where everyone could keep an eye on you.'

'I don't want to go back!' I burst out.

Mum narrowed her eyes at me. 'What did they do to you there, then?'

'It was *awful*!' I launched in. 'They kept locking me in the quiet room if I did the slightest little thing and everyone kept picking on me. I got blamed for everything. And there was this big girl, Justine, she kept beating me up. Though I beat her up too. And we played this Dare Game and I was *heaps* more daring than she was. I ran all round the garden of the Children's Home without any clothes on and Justine only ate one worm but I ate two really wriggly ones—'

'Hey hey, you're a right little nutter, you are! They're not a good influence, children's homes. Still, don't worry, you're not going back.'

'So . . . am I going to stay with Cam?'

Mum put her head on one side. 'Don't you want to come and live with me?'

I stared at her. I stared and stared and stared. I wanted to rewind her so that I could hear her all over again. And again. I couldn't believe it. Or was she kidding? 'Really? With you, Mum?'

'That's what I said.'

'For how long? A whole week?' I asked.

'Never mind a week! How about for ever?'

'Wow!' She still had her fag so I didn't jump on her. I jumped on Elaine's swivel chair instead and whirled it round and round.

'Don't do that, you're doing my head in,' said Mum.

I stopped, sharpish.

'It's time we got together, darling,' she said softly. 'I've missed my little girl so much. We're going to make a go of it together, just you and me.'

It was like she'd taken me by the hand and we were climbing a golden staircase right up into the sky. And then I tripped on a step because I suddenly thought of something.

'But what about Cam?'

'What about her?' said Mum. She took a last drag and then squashed her cigarette fiercely inside the Bunnikins mug. I imagined all their powder-puff tails scorching. 'Never mind this Cam. She's not family. Oh, Tracy, we'll have such a great time together. First we'll kit you out with some new clothes, smarten you up a little—'

'I'll smarten up all you want, Mum, no

worries on that score. Designer clothes?'

'Only the best for my girl. None of this shabby chainstore stuff. You don't want to look the same as all the other kids. You want to look that bit *special*.'

'You bet!' I whirled round one more time. 'Genuine logos, not fake market stuff?'

'Who do you think I am?' said Mum, hands on hips.

'You're my *mum*,' I said.

S-o-o-o-o . . . I'm going to have my fairytale happy ending and more than half this notebook is still empty! I'm going to live with my mum. I am. I am. Just as soon as we've got it sorted out with Elaine.

'I'll sort her!' said Mum.

And of course there's Cam.

Cam.

Alexander's Home

I'm mad at Cam. I mean, I went through agonies telling her. I felt really bad. I was nearly crying. I thought it would be awful for her. But do you know something? She didn't seem to care at all! She didn't gasp and cry and cling to me. She just sat there, biting her nails, though she ticks me off something rotten if I do that. She didn't say anything. Not a single word. No 'Don't leave me, darling Tracy, you mean the whole world to me and I can't live without you.' Nothing.

So I got a bit mad then and told her that my mum thinks I look a right old scruffbag and she's going to get me kitted out in a full set of designer clothes. I thought *that* might get her going. I thought she might say, 'Oh, Tracy, I feel so bad, I've never given you decent clothes, but tell you what, if you promise to stay with me we'll go into town right away and I'll wave my credit card like a wand and you can wear anything you want, money no object, just so long as you live with me.' But not a bit of it. She still said a big fat NOTHING.

So I got really *really* mad because she obviously couldn't care less so I went on about all this other stuff my mum was going to buy me, like a computer and rollerblades and a new bike and a trip to Disneyland and she didn't even flinch. Didn't try to compete. Simply couldn't be bothered. She just sat there, nibble nibble on her nails, like she was bored with the whole situation and couldn't wait to be shot of me.

So *then* I was so mega-mad I just wanted to don Doc Martens and jump up and down on her so I went on and on about my mum and how great she is and fantastically beautiful and wonderfully dressed and how we had these amazing cuddles and it was just like we'd never ever been parted.

And she *still* didn't say a word! Nibble

nibble on the nails till she was nearly down to her own knuckles.

'Say something!'

She just sat there and sat there and then she eventually took her hand out of her mouth and mumbled, 'I don't really know what to say.'

Call herself a *writer*!

'I thought you were meant to be good with words!'

'Just at the moment they're sticking in my throat,' she mumbled, like I'd just squirted Superglue round her tonsils.

I went and stood right in front of her. She was all huddled up, almost as if I *had* been jumping all over her. I had this sharp little pain in my chest. I suddenly felt like *I* was the mother and she was my little girl. 'You're sad, aren't you, Cam?' I said softly.

She made more mumbly noises and started nail-biting again.

I reached out and took hold of her nibbled hand. 'You're unhappy that my mum's come back, aren't you?' I said hopefully.

Cam didn't say anything for a few seconds. Then she gave me this weird smile, practically stretching from ear to ear. 'I'm happy for you, Tracy,' she said.

I dropped her hand like it was red hot and ran out of the room.

Happy! Smiling all over her face!

She obviously couldn't wait to be rid of me. She doesn't care about me at all. Well, *I* don't care. I don't need her. I've got my mum now.

I'll go and live with Mum and I shan't mind a bit if I never see Cam ever again. I'm not going to take any notice of her. I'm just going to put my life on hold until I can go and live with my mum. I'm not going to go to school either.

I'm in a bit of bother at school at the moment. I started up the Dare Game, quite by chance. Roxanne was calling me the B word again because she knows it really gets to me, so I dared her to say it in front of Mrs Bagley.

I thought she'd chicken out. But her eyes glittered and she said, 'Right!' She marched right up to Mrs V.B. and said, 'Tracy Beaker told me to say this weird word, Mrs Bagley,' and then she said it straight out and added, all Little Miss Innocence, 'Is it *rude*?'

So guess who got into trouble.

'And *I* won the dare,' said Roxanne.

I stuck my tongue out at her, waggling it as rudely as I could.

'It's my turn to dare you now,' said Roxanne. 'I dare you to stick your tongue out like that at Mrs Bagley!'

So I did. And guess who got into trouble again.

'But it's my turn now,' I said, catching up with Roxanne at break. I peered past the cloakrooms and had a sudden inspiration. 'OK, I dare you to run right into the boys' toilets!'

So she did. But she said I'd pushed her in. So I got into heaps more trouble.

And now it was her turn to dare me. She waited till lunchtime. It was spaghetti bolognaise. I don't like school spag bol. The cook makes it bright red like blood and the spaghetti seems extra wiggly like worms. I pushed my plateful away from me.

'Don't you want it, Tracy?' said Roxanne, her eyes going glitter glitter glitter. 'OK, I dare you to tip it over your head!'

So I did. And when Roxanne and all her

stupid friends started screaming with laughter I tipped Roxanne's spag bol over *her* head.

I ended up in BIG BIG BIG trouble. I had to stand outside the head's office for the rest of the day in Total Disgrace. Mr Hatherway went past and shook his head at me. 'Hair ribbon?' he said, picking a strand of spaghetti out of my curls. 'It looks like you've really hit the jackpot today, Tracy. What's poor Mrs Bagley going to do with you, eh?'

I was sure she was going to invent some serious form of torture.

I don't see why I should submit to serious Vomit Bag Aggro. I won't even go in for registration. What do I care if they phone up Cam and complain? I shan't be at that school much longer. My mum will send me to a brand-new super school where I'll be dead popular because of all my designer clothes and everyone will be in awe of me and be desperate to be my best friend and even the teachers will think I'm the greatest and I'll be top of the class and the best girl in the whole school.

You wait.

You just wait and see.

So when Cam took me to school this morning I waved goodbye and ran into the playground – and went on running, all round the kids and then back out again and down the road, running and running, and I kept it up for ages, acting like there were Tracy-catchers prowling with  nets and hooks and manacles. I didn't know why I was running like crazy.

Then I realized where I was running to. My house.

I rounded the corner – and a football came whizzing straight through the air, about to knock my head clean off my shoulders. But I'm Tracy-SuperStar, the girl-goalie with nanosecond-quick reactions. I leapt, I clutched, I tucked the ball close to my chest – *saved*!

'Wow!' I yelled, congratulating myself.

This big burly kid came charging up, his

head as round as the football but with little prickles all over, a serious don't-mess-with-me haircut. Make that hair*shave*.

'Give us that ball,' he said.

'Did you see the way I caught it?' I said, leaping about. 'What a save, eh?'

'Sheer fluke,' said the Football guy. He knocked the ball out of my hand and started dribbling with it.

'Sheer *skill*!' I said indignantly. 'Come on, see if you can get another ball past me.'

'I don't play with girls.'

'Girls are great at footie,' I said. 'Well, *I* am. Let's play, yeah?'

'No! Get lost, little girly.'

I suddenly charged at him. He stiffened in surprise, expecting some kind of mad attack – and forgot about his ball. I gave it a nifty little hooking kick and whipped it right out of his reach.

'Superb tackle!' I yelled, nudging it along. 'The great Tracy Beaker and her brilliant footwork yet again. She's really come good, this girl – OUCH!'

Football did not tackle back with finesse.

He went whack. I went smack. On my back.

I lay there, groaning. Football stopped, bouncing the ball right by my head. 'You all right, kid?' he said.

'Oh yeah. Sure. Just having a little kip on the pavement,' I mumbled.

'I didn't mean to knock you flying like that. I didn't realize you're such a little kid.'

'I'm not!' I said, insulted.

'Here.' He reached out with his great pink hand and suddenly I was hauled upright. 'OK now? Mind you, it's your own fault. You shouldn't have messed around with my football.'

'I wasn't messing, I was tackling! You've got a totally useless defence. Here –' I gave a sudden lunge, all set to prove my point, but he was wise to me now and got the ball well away before I could get near it.

'Give over, kid!' he said, laughing – and then he dribbled the ball round the corner.

'Don't go! Hey, Football, come back. Play with me, eh? There isn't anyone else. Go on. Football?'

But he'd gone.

'See if I care. You're lousy at football anyway,' I yelled.

Then I sloped off. To the house. I decided it was definitely going to be *my* house. Until I go off and live with Mum and have my very own *real* house.

I'd not got the cushion and the blanket organized. Or any proper provisions. I searched my pockets for forgotten goodies. The best I could do was an ancient chewed piece of gum stuck in the corner of a tissue. Well, I *think* it was gum. Certainly it didn't look very appetizing, whatever. I didn't have any cash on me either. It looked like I was going to have to play skinny-starving-to-death-fashion-model in my house – not my most favourite game.

But the weirdest thing happened. I went up the scruffy path at the back, investigating an old Kentucky Chicken carton with my foot just in case. (No luck at all, totally licked clean to the bone.) I climbed in through the back window, negotiated the kitchen, and walked into the living room, my footsteps sounding oddly loud on the bare floorboards. The old curtains were drawn so it was quite dark in the room, but I could still see my red velvet sofa in the middle of the room . . . with

76

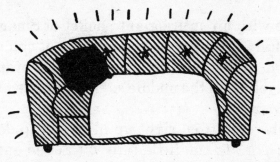

a big black velvet cushion at one end and a blue blanket neatly covering the worst of the muddy marks.

I stared at them as if I'd conjured them out of thin air. It was like one of those old fairy-tales. I squinted long and hard at the cushion and the blanket to see if they were being toted about by disembodied hands. I liked this idea even if it was kind of spooky. Maybe the hands were perched in a corner somewhere ready to flap their flying fingers at my command?

'OK, the cushion and the blanket are spot on, but what about some *food*?' I said, snapping my own fingers.

Then I stopped mid-snap, my nails digging into my thumbs. I'd spotted an upturned card-board packing case over by the window, with a checked dishcloth neatly laid over it like a little tablecloth. There was a paper party plate with an entire giant packet of Smarties carefully arranged on top in rings of colour – brown, green, blue, mauve, pink, red, orange, with yellow in the middle so that it looked like a flower.

I shivered from right up in the scalp down  to the little taily bit at the end of my spine. My favourite food in all the world is Smarties. And here was a big plate of them beautifully laid out just for me.

'It *is* magic!' I whispered, and I circled the cardboard table.

I put out a hand and picked up a red Smartie. I licked it. It was real. I popped it in my mouth, and then hurriedly shoved another handful after it in case they suddenly disappeared. Then I went to draw the old dusty curtains so I could have a closer look and suss out how this magic was working.

AAAHHHH!!!

I yanked at the curtain – and screamed. Someone else screamed too!

A boy was sitting scrunched up on the window ledge, knees up under his little pointy chin,

hands clasping a book, mouth gasping, eyes
blink-blink-blinking.

'What are you *doing* here? Are you trying
to frighten me?' I yelled.

He clasped his book so tightly it was in
danger of buckling. His eyes were little slits
because his face was so screwed up. 'You
frightened *me*,' he whispered.

'What are you doing in my house?' I
demanded.

He sat up a little straighter. 'It's my house,
actually,' he said timidly.

'You don't live here.'

'Yes I do. Well, during the day I do. I'm
making it my home. I brought the cushion.
And the rug. And organized refreshments.'

'You what? Oh. The Smarties.'

He looked over at the plate. 'You spoilt my
pattern,' he said.

'It's only babies who play with food. Well,
that's what they said at the Children's Home
when I made my peas climb up my mashed
potato mountain.'

'Did you really think it was magic?' he
asked.

'Of course not!' I said firmly.

'I thought by the sound of your footsteps

you were really big and scary,' he said, un-clenching and swinging his legs free. 'That's why I hid.'

'I *am* big and scary,' I said. 'Bigger than you, anyway, you little squirt.'

'Everyone's bigger than me,' he said humbly.

'How old are you then? Nine? Ten?'

'I'm nearly twelve!'

I stared. 'You don't look it!'

'I know.'

'So what are you doing here then?' I asked, helping myself to another handful of Smarties. I offered him the plate, seeing as they were his refresh-ments. He said thank you politely and ate one blue Smartie, nibbling at the edges first like it was a biscuit. He didn't answer me.

'Are you bunking off?' I asked.

He hesitated, then nodded. 'You won't tell, will you?' he said, swallowing his Smartie.

'I'm not a snitch.' I looked him up and down. 'Fancy you bunking off! You look too much of a goody-goody teacher's pet. Dead swotty!' I pointed to his big fat book, trying to work out the title. 'Alex-an-der the Great. The great what?'

'No, that was just what they called him.'

'As in Tracy the Great?' I rather liked the sound of it. 'That's me. Tracy.'

'I'm Alexander,' he said.

'Ah. Alexander the not-so-great. So. You're obviously dead brainy. Why do you need to bunk off? I bet you come top of everything.'

He nodded. 'Yep. Except for PE. I'm bottom at PE. I always bunk off on games days.'

'You're mad. PE's a bit of a laugh. Especially when it's football.'

I'm truly Tracy the Great at footie, famed for my nippy footwork and dirty tackles. Old Vomit Bagley goes bright red in the face blowing her whistle at me.

Alexander was whingeing on about them being even worse then.

'Them?'

'The other boys. They tease me.'

'What about?'

Alexander ducked his head. 'All sorts of stuff. Especially . . . when we're in the showers.'

'Aha!'

'They laugh at me because . . .'

'Because you're Alexander the not-so-great!' I said, giggling.

Alexander flinched as if I'd hit him. I suddenly felt mean. I hitched myself up on the window seat beside him. 'So you bunk off?' I said.

'Mmm.'

'Haven't they complained to your mum?'

'Yes.'

'So what did she say?'

'She never says anything much. It's Dad.' Alexander said the word 'Dad' as if it meant Rottweiler.

'What did *he* say?'

I could feel Alexander trembling. 'He said – he said – he said he'd send me away to boarding school if I didn't watch out, and then I couldn't play truant. And he said I'd *really* get bullied there.'

'He sounds dead caring, your dad,' I said, and I patted Alexander on his bony little shoulder.

'He says I have to learn to stand up for myself.'

I snorted and suddenly gave him the teeniest little push. He squealed in shock and nearly fell off the window seat. I hauled him back. 'You're not even very good at *sitting* up for yourself,'

I said, shaking my head at him.

'I know,' Alexander said dolefully.

'So come on then. Try fighting back.'

'I can't. I don't know how.'

'I'll show you.'

He was in luck. I'm the greatest fighter in the world. I'm especially good at getting a sly punch in first. And I don't just rely on fists. I'm great at kicking shins. If I'm really pushed I bare my killer choppers and bite.

I pulled Alexander off the window seat and tried to get him to put his fists up. His little hands drooped back down to his sides.

'I can't fight. And anyway, I can't hit a girl.'

'You won't get a chance, matey,' I said, putting my own fists up. I gave him one little gentle punch. Then another. He didn't react, apart from blinking rapidly.

'Come on! Try to hit me back.'

Alexander lunged at me feebly. His fist could have been cotton wool.

'Harder!'

He had one more go. I stepped sideways and he punched thin air, stumbled, and very nearly fell over.

'Oh well. I see what you mean,' I said,

realizing he was a totally hopeless case.

'I'm useless,' said Alexander, drooping all over.

'Only at fighting,' I said. I pondered. I looked at his funny little feet in their highly polished Clarks lace-ups. It didn't look like he'd be much of a kicker. His tiny teeth only seemed capable of a hamster nibble, not a vicious vampire bite. Other tactics might be required. I tried to think what I did those rare times when I was up against some huge gorilla guy who could jump up and down all over me. Easy. I got lippy (and then ran).

'See this,' I said to Alexander, and I stuck out my tongue. It is a very long pink tongue and I can waggle it till I almost touch my ears. Alexander backed away nervously. I replaced my tongue with pride. 'It's more cutting than the sharpest knife.'

Alexander nodded in agreement. I wondered if he got what I meant.

'You want to say something really cutting to those boys at your school.'

'Oh *sure*,' said Alexander. I detected a surprising spot of sarcasm. 'Then they'd beat me up even more.'

Maybe he had a point.

'So why don't you say something to make them laugh? Like when you're in the showers?'

'They laugh at me already.'

'Make them laugh *more*.' I thought hard, trying to imagine myself into the situation. I got the giggles. 'I know!' I snorted. 'You tell them they might all have zonking great cucumbers but you're very happy with your own little gherkin.'

Alexander blinked at me. 'I can't say that!'

'Yes you can.'

'I wouldn't dare.'

'Yes you would. *I* dare you. There. Now you've got to say it. If you want to be my friend.'

Alexander looked puzzled. 'Are we friends?'

The cheek of it!

'Don't you want to be friends?' I demanded.

Alexander nodded. Wisely.

'Right. So we're friends. And we'll meet up again tomorrow?' I said.

Same time. Same place. He'd better be there. I hope he organizes some more refreshments.

Football's Home

It was a little bit dodgy getting away. Cam came over all stroppy about school and the fact that I've been bunking off. Not that I *told* her. I'm not into that True Confession lark. But the head phoned her up to tell her little Tracy was conspicuously absent and Cam got seriously fussed.

She started giving me a l-o-n-g lecture and I just happened to give the teeniest little yawn. Cam caught hold of me by the shoulders so I had to look at her. 'Tracy, this is serious.'

'Yeah, yeah.'

'I mean it.' Her silly short hair was sticking up all over the place. I can't see why she can't grow her hair into a decent style. She'd look so much better if she wore make-up too. I don't know why she doesn't want to make herself look pretty. Like my mum.

I didn't really want to look at her. I blinked so that my eyes went blurry and I just mumbled 'Mmm.' Then I wriggled. 'You're digging into my shoulders, Cam.'

She looked like she really wanted to dig straight through my skin but she just nodded and let me go. 'It *is* serious, Trace. You keep on and you'll be excluded.'

'Wow! Really?'

That Football guy is excluded. It only happens to the really tough nuts. I rather fancy being the Toughest Nutter of all.

'Don't sound so hopeful!'

'It's mad – you bunk off school because you hate it and they get narked and threaten you with this huge punishment, No School At All, which is *precisely* what you want most in the world!'

'You don't really *hate* school, do you?'

'Oh per-lease!'

'I know you don't get on very well with Mrs Bagley.'

'Understatement of the century!'

'But you won't be stuck in her class for ever. You're bright; if you'd only give it a chance you could do really well, pass all your exams—'

'I don't need to pass exams to be an actress.'

'I thought you wanted to be a writer.'

'I've changed my mind. I'd much sooner be an actress.'

'Like your mum?'

'Yep.'

I went off into a little dream, thinking about Mum and how it was going to be. Maybe I  could get into acting straight away and we could be in films together, a real mother and daughter act: Mum could play my mum – not as a Mumsie type, naturally, more sexy and sassy – and I could be this cute kid with a sharp line in wisecracks. I could just see it.

'Tracy –' Cam's voice interfered with my imaginary reception. 'I know you love your mum very much. It's great you've been able to see her again. But maybe – maybe it might be better not to pin all your hopes on your mum.'

I knew what she was getting at. I didn't want to listen. I've got so many hopes pinned on my mum she's like a human pin-cushion.

It's going to be all right. We're going to be OK, Mum and me. We are we are we are. I'm going to stay with her next weekend and I can't *wait*.

Do you know something? Cam still doesn't seem to mind a bit. 'If it's what you want, Tracy,' she said.

'Of course it's what I want. But what do *you* want?'

'What I want is for you to stop playing truant. I want you to promise you won't bunk off school tomorrow. Or the next day. Or the next. Ever again. Promise, Tracy.'

I promised. With my fingers crossed behind my back. It doesn't matter. Cam doesn't keep promises herself. I mean, she was all set for it to be me and her together for ever. And yet now my mum's come back on the scene Cam acts like she can't wait to be rid of me. Well, see if I care.

My mum's *desperate* to get me back. She's FANTASTIC. Even better than I made up. The best mum in the world.

She is.

She IS.

90

Better than anyone else's. *Cam's* mum is this weird old posh lady who lives in the country somewhere and doesn't want to see Cam any more because she disapproves of her lifestyle.

Alexander's mum sounds like this little mouse who squeaks in a corner and shivers whenever his dad stalks past.

Football's mum is just the opposite, fiercer than fierce, and *foul*.

I saw her today when I bunked off school. I *had* to see if Alexander followed through with his dare. I went to the Spar on the corner first to fork out for a few refreshments with my school dinner money. I was wandering back up the road when I saw this woman coming out of her house yelling back into the hall, 'You can get out of your bed, you lazy great slummock, and get cracking with that vacuuming or you'll be for it when I get home. Did you hear me? I said, DID YOU HEAR ME?'

You could hear her all the way up and down the street. People were probably wincing and putting their hands over their ears the other side of town. She had a voice like a car alarm, going on and on and on, so loud and insistent it was like it was ringing inside your head as well as out.

'And if you dare get into one more spot of bother then I'm telling you straight, I'm having you put away. I'm sick to death of you, do you hear me? You're rubbish. No use to anyone. Just like your rotten father.'

She slammed the door and went slapping down the path in her grubby trainers, her huge thighs wobbling in her old leggings.

The upstairs window opened and the Football boy stuck his head out. He was in his vest, still all sleepy-eyed, straight from his bed, but he was still cradling his football.

'Don't you call my dad rotten!' he yelled.

'Don't get lippy with me, you lousy little whatsit!' she screamed. 'And don't you *dare* start sticking up for your lazy lying slug of a father!'

'Stop it! Don't call him names! He's worth ten of you!' Football shouted, going bright red in the face.

'You think you know it all, eh? Staying in your bed half the day, never helping out, mucking things up at school, in trouble with the old Bill – yeah, you've really got your life worked out, my son.'

'I wish I wasn't your son. I wish I lived with my dad.'

'Oh right. OK then. Off you go. Live with him, why don't you?'

Football's face got even redder. 'Yeah. Well. I would,' he mumbled.

'But he don't want you, right?' she yelled triumphantly. 'Face up to it, son. He's got his silly little lady friend – although by God she's no lady – and so he doesn't want me and he doesn't want you either, for all he goes on about you being best mates. He couldn't wait to turn his back on you – and he hasn't come back, has he?'

'He's taking me to the match on Saturday!'

'Oh yeah? Like he was a fortnight ago? He doesn't give a stuff about you.'

'He does, he does!' Football yelled, and there were tears dribbling down his bright red cheeks.

'You pathetic little cry-baby!' his mum jeered.

Football took aim. His football went flying through the air and landed wallop, right on her head. He cheered tearfully as she swore, words so bad they'd burn right through the page if I wrote them down.

Then she stopped rubbing her head and grabbed hold of his football. 'Right!' she said, and she kicked it way way way over the rooftops out of sight. I suppose she'd have made a seriously good footballer herself. Then *she* cheered.

'That's fixed *you*,' she said, and she marched off. She nearly bumped into me as she went. 'Had a good gawp, have you?' she said, pushing me out the way. 'Nosy little whatsit!'

I told her I wouldn't hurt my eyes gawping at something as ugly as her. Well, I whispered it. I didn't quite want to get into a shouting match with her myself.

Football was shouting too. At me. Telling me to clear off and mind my own business. Or words to that effect. Almost as bad as his mum.

He wiped his face very quickly so that I couldn't see the tears. Though I'd already seen them, of course. But I cleared off and ate most of my tube of Smarties to calm myself because I can't stick it if people start yelling and screaming – unless it's me. Then I made for the house and you'll never guess what! *There* was the football, in the garden, landed smack in a soggy carton of sweet and sour sauce. Now that had to be magic! I mean, fancy that football landing in *my* garden!

So I decided to be a good little fairy myself. I picked the football up gingerly and wiped all the orange goo off on the grass and bounced it all the way back to Football's house.

I banged at his door.

No answer.

I banged again.

Nothing. I stared at the peeling paint, wondering if I'd got the wrong house. No, I was pretty sure. I backed down the garden path and peered up at the window.

'Oi – you! Football guy!' I bellowed. 'Want

your ball back?' I bounced it hard to show I wasn't kidding.

It worked! The window went up and Football's head poked out. 'What are you doing with my ball?' he bellowed, as if *I'd* been the one to kick it over the rooftops.

'OK, pal, if you're not even *grateful* . . .' I said, and I turned my back and went bouncy-bouncy-bouncy to his gate.

'Wait!' he yelled.

I knew he would. He came charging out in two ticks in his vest and tracksuit bottoms and bare feet. Those little pink wiggly toes made him look much less fierce.

'Give us it then,' he said.

'Play a game of footie with me?'

'I told you before, I don't play with girls.'

'Then I'll take this ball and find some guy who *will* play with me,' I said.

He tried to tackle me then, but I was too quick for him.

'You little . . .' More *amazing* words.

'You haven't half got a mouth on you. You obviously take after your mum.'

That *really* got him going. Blank blank blankety blank, you blanking blanker.

'Hasn't anyone ever washed your mouth out with soap?' I said.

'Ha ha,' he said, not laughing. He was eyeing the ball, but I kept it out of his reach.

'They used to do it in the Children's Home. This careworker shoved a great cake of her Body Shop Dewberry soap right in my gob when I was just the weeniest bit lippy. It was *disgusting*. Still, I bit it into pieces so she couldn't use it any more. And then I was sick and she got scared in case I reported her for abuse. The sick was all foamy. It looked pretty impressive.'

Football was looking at me like he was a little impressed himself. 'You've been in care?' he said.

'Sure,' I said. 'Still am. Technically. Though any minute now I'm getting back with my mum. She's the most amazing actress and she's incredibly beautiful and she thinks I'll make it in the movies too and—'

And Football tackled me and got the ball back, laughing.

'You rotten . . .' My own language sparkled and hissed too.

I thought he'd go back indoors with his blooming ball and slam the door on me, but he hung around on his doorstep, heading the ball at the front wall, backwards and forwards.

'So, what's it like then?' he said, a little breathlessly because he was really whacking that ball. It made my eyes smart to watch him.

'What's what like? Hey, give me a go at heading it, eh?'

'You've got to be joking!'

'You're so mean! I got you your rotten ball back.'

'I don't think it's mine anyway.' Football caught it and swivelled it around. 'I had my name inked on it, plus a dire warning of what I'd do if anyone got their dirty mitts on it.'

'So it's really not yours?'

'Never mind. It's actually in better nick. I'd really hammered my last one.'

'Then it's just as much mine as yours – so give it here!'

'OK, OK, I'll play five minutes' footie with you – *after* you tell me what it's like to be in care.'

'What do you want to know for?'

'Because my mum keeps threatening stuff, see – and then I've got this social worker—'

'So have I. Elaine the Pain!' I pulled a face.

'What did you get up to then, a little kid like you?'

'I've been up to *all* sorts,' I boasted.

'But you haven't really been in trouble with the old Bill. I have. Lots,' said Football, swaggering.

'Yeah well. *I've* been too clever to get caught,' I said.

'So what *is* it like? Do they really beat you with wet towels so you don't get bruises? And do the older ones bash the little ones up and stick their heads down the toilets? And do the boys have to wear short trousers even in winter so they're a laughing stock? My mum says—'

Aha! I decided to wind him up just a tiny bit. 'That's right! Only it's far worse,' I said. 'The food's awful, all these meat loaves made of cow's nostrils and uddery bits, so you get mad cow disease as *well* as being sick. And *if* you're sick at a meal they pile it up on a plate and make you eat it.'

Football was staring at me, eyes popping, mouth open, like he was about to be sick himself. I could have nicked his ball – *my* ball – there and then, but this seemed like more fun. I went on elaborating and he carried on drinking it all in and it wasn't until I invented this torture chamber where they keep you handcuffed in the dark and let live rats run all over you and burrow down beneath your underwear that he suddenly twigged.

'You're having me on!' he said. He stared at me, his face scrunching up. I decided I might have to back off sharpish. But then this weird spluttery noise started up. Old Football was laughing!

'You're a weird little kid! OK, OK, I'll play footie with you. But just for five minutes, right?'

He went into his house to put on a T-shirt. He left the door ajar so I followed him in. It wasn't much cop at all. The carpet was all fraying at the edges and covered in bits. I could see why his mum had nagged on about the vacuuming. It looked like the whole house needed spring-cleaning. There were scuffs and marks all over the walls – obviously traces of Football's football.

He was in his living room, shoving his feet into his trainers. 'Here, you. I didn't ask you in.'

'I know. But I'm dead nosy. Seeing as I haven't got a real home.'

Football's certainly wasn't my idea of home sweet home. Yesterday's takeaways were congealing on trays by the sofa. The ashtray was so full it was spilling over and the whole room smelt stale. It was *empty* too. Well, there was a sofa and chairs and the telly, but that was about it. Cam's got all her cushions and patchwork and plants and pictures all over the walls and books in piles and little ornaments and vases of dried flowers and windchimes and notebooks and painted boxes and this daft old donkey she had when she was little. She said I could have Daisy if I wanted. I said I wasn't a silly little kid who played with toy animals. Cam said good, because she

was a silly little woman who still liked
cuddling up with Daisy when she was feeling
dead depressed and she didn't really want to
give her away.

I've tried hanging onto the old donkey once
or twice, when Cam's not
around. Daisy's got this old
soft woolly smell, and the
insides of her big ears are all
velvety.

You can't cuddle up with anything at all
in Football's house. Maybe Football doesn't
mind. He's certainly not a cuddly kind
of guy.

We played football out in
the street. It was great for a
bit.

But then these other
guys came sloping past
and Football acted like I was this
little bee buzzing in his ear.
He swotted me away
and started playing football
with these other guys.

'Hey, what about me?'
I demanded indignantly.

'You push off now,' Football hissed out the side of his mouth, like he couldn't even bear to be seen talking to me.

'OK, OK. But you give me back my ball. I found it. And you said it wasn't yours.'

I got into a bit of an argument about it. Football and his new mates won.

I decided I didn't want to play footie with him if he were the last guy in the world. In fact, I'd gone off the game altogether so there was no point taking my ball with me. So I didn't insist.

I sloped off to the old house to see Alexander. I needed to see if he'd followed my advice and learned to stick up for himself.

Tracy and Alexander's Home

I let myself in the back window and noted straight away that someone had been making serious improvements in the kitchen. There was a big bottle of mineral water standing on the draining board, with a label saying THIS IS THE TAP. So I drank a little 'tap' water because Football (and the ensuing dispute) had been thirsty work. I slurped a little down my T-shirt but there was a clean towel hanging on a hook so I could mop myself up. A cardboard box was stacked in a corner with another label: THIS IS THE FRIDGE. I inspected the 'fridge' contents with interest. I discovered two rounds of tuna sandwiches, a packet of cheese and onion crisps, a Kit-Kat and an apple. *Plus* a giant pack of Smarties!!! I helped myself to a handful or two because I'd already burnt up a lot of energy that morning. I was all set to share my own refreshments – only I'd somehow or other eaten them up. Still, I was sure Alexander would be happy to share *his* refreshments with me.

'Alexander?' I called. It came out indistinctly, because my mouth was full. I tried again, louder. '*Alexander?*'

I heard a little mousy squeak from the living room. Alexander was sitting cross-legged on a little rug in front of another cardboard box. There was a drawing of smiley *Blue Peter* presenters on the front and another label: THIS IS THE TELEVISION.

'It seems to be on permanent freeze-frame,' I said wittily.

Alexander seemed unusually immobile too, hunched up with his chin on his chest.

'Are you OK?' I asked, sitting down beside him.

'Yes,' he said. Then, 'Well, no, not really.'

'Ah,' I said. 'What's up, then?'

Alexander sighed heavily. 'Everything,' he said sadly, and went back to watching the frozen TV programme.

'How did you get on at school?' I asked.

He didn't react, though his eyes flicked backwards and forwards as if the presenters were really doing something on the screen.

'You know, with the big bully boys in the showers?'

Alexander sighed again and slumped even further into his shoulders. 'The entire school calls me Gherkin now.'

I couldn't help spluttering. Alexander looked at me as if I'd kicked him.

'Sorry. *Sorry!* It just . . . sounded funny.'

'Everyone thinks it's very funny. Except me.'

'Oh dear. Well. Never mind.'

'I do mind. Dreadfully.'

'Still.' I struggled hard to say something optimistic. 'At least you won the dare. I dared you to do it, didn't I? And you did. So you get to win that dare.'

'Big deal,' said Alexander.

I thought hard. 'OK. You get to dare me now.'

'I don't really want to, thank you.'

I couldn't believe his attitude. Didn't he realize the potential of my offer??? 'Go *on*, Alexander,' I said impatiently, standing over him.

Alexander wriggled backwards on his bony bottom. 'I can't make up any dares,' he said meekly. 'You make one up, Tracy.'

'Don't be so wet! Come on. Dare me to do something really really wicked.'

Alexander thought hard. Then I saw light in his pale blue eyes. 'All right. I dare you to . . . I dare you to . . . stand on your head.'

He just didn't *get* it! But I decided to show willing. I spat on my hands and sprang forward. 'Easy-peasy,' I said, upside down.

'Gosh! You're really good at it.'

'Anyone can stand on their head.'

'I can't.'

I might have known. I tried hard to show him. He was useless. He just crumpled in a heap whenever he tried to kick his legs up.

'Watch *me*!' I said, doing headstands and handstands and then a cartwheel round the room.

'I can see your knickers,' said Alexander, giggling.

'Well, don't look,' I said breathlessly.

'I can't help it,' said Alexander. Then he started singing this weird song about leaping up and down and waving your knickers in the air.

'You what?' I said, right way up again.

'It's a song,' said Alexander. 'My dad sings it when he's in a good mood. Which isn't often when I'm around.' He sang it again.

'Is that another dare?' I said.

Alexander giggled.

'Right!' I said, and I whipped my knickers off and leapt up and down, waving them like a flag.

'Tracy! Um! You are *rude*!' Alexander spluttered, nearly keeling over sideways he was laughing so much.

I leapt right round the cardboard television, waving away, and pranced past the window.

'Tracy! Get away from the window! Someone will see,' Alexander screeched.

'I don't care,' I said, bouncing up and down as if the bare floorboards were a trampoline. 'Look at me, everyone! Look at m-e-e-e!'

A football suddenly came flying through the window and bounced right across the floor. Alexander must have seen it coming but he didn't duck in time. It caught him bang on the bonce.

'Ouch! A football!' he said, rubbing his head.

'*My* football,' I said, retrieving it triumphantly.

'Who on earth threw it in here?' said Alexander.

I didn't need three guesses. Football himself came climbing through the window. It's a harder window to negotiate than the one in the kitchen at the back. He jumped down, lost his balance, stumbled forward . . . and landed on Alexander.

Alexander lay quivering, hands over his head.

'You clumsy great oaf!' I said to Football. 'Are you all right, Alexander?'

'No,' said Alexander, whimpering.

Football picked him up and brushed him down. 'Yes you are,' he said firmly.

'Bully,' I said, bouncing the ball one-handed. 'First you beat me up. And I'm a girl and I'm younger than you. And then you pick on a total wimp like Alexander.'

I was *defending* Alexander but he crumpled again at the word wimp. I sighed. There's something about Alexander that kind of makes you *want* to bully him. Even though you know it's mean.

'Bully, bully, bully,' I said, bouncing the ball in time.

'Give me my ball back, kid,' said Football.

'It's *my* ball.'

'You gave it to me.'

'And then I took it back. It's my ball now. And this is *my* house and you're not invited so you can just clear off. What are you doing following me, anyway?'

'I didn't follow you. I was just checking up

111

on you. And it's not *your* house.'

'It is, it is, it is,' I said, bouncing.

'It's my house too,' said Alexander.

I smiled at him and bounced the ball to him. An easy-peasy bounce but he totally misjudged it. His hands closed on thin air and the ball bounced past. Football stuck out a paw and caught the ball.

'Alexander!' I said.

Alexander hung his head.

'*My* ball now,' said Football, smirking. He started bouncing so hard the cardboard furniture vibrated.

'You'll break the television,' said Alexander.

'You what?' said Football.

'You're interfering with the reception, look,' said Alexander.

I twigged that he was deliberately distracting him. I grinned – and as Football peered in disbelief at the cardboard box I whipped the ball from his arms. I used two hands – and Something fell on the floor. Football peered hard at the Something.

'I've got the ball, I've got the ball' I gabbled quickly, to distract him again.

This time it didn't work. Football bent over,

grinning, and picked up the
Something with his thumb and
forefinger. 'What's this, then?'
he said, grinning.

'Nothing,' I said. Though it obviously
wasn't Nothing. It was a pretty embarrassing
Something.

'It's your knickers!' Football chortled.

'She's been leaping up and down and
waving her knickers in the air.'

'Shut *up*, Alexander,' I said furiously.

I snatched my knickers back and stuffed
them in my pocket.

Football laughed loudly and made an
extremely coarse remark. I told him to watch
his mouth and he said I should watch his
ball – as he knocked it out
of my arms. He
cheered himself
wildly and then
kicked the ball
all round the living
room, knocking the
television over and severely denting the table.

'Do you mind! This is my living room, not a
football pitch,' I said.

'It's my living room too,' said Alexander,

quickly dodging out of Football's way.

'I've got just as much right to be here as you have. And I say it's not a dopey old living room, it's a cracking indoor football pitch,' said Football, but this time he dribbled the ball carefully *round* the furniture, keeping up a running commentary all the time:

'Yeah, our boy's got the ball again, ready to save the day . . . *yes*, he intercepts the ball brilliantly, heading it s-t-r-a-i-g-h-t' (he took aim as he gabbled and suddenly kicked it hard against the wall) 'into the net! *Yes!*' (He punched the air.) 'I've never seen such a brilliant goal.'

'Sad,' I said to Alexander, shaking my head.

'You wait till I'm famous,' said Football, kicking the ball in my direction. Aiming *at* me, rather than to me.

But I'm no weedy Alexander. I stood my ground and kicked it straight back. 'Wow! Tracy's a gutsy little player!' I commentated. 'I bet I'm heaps more famous than you anyway.'

'Women footballers are rubbish,' said Football.

'I'm not going to be a footballer, you nutcase. I'm going to be a famous actress like my mum.'

'Now who's sad?' Football said to Alexander. He bounced the ball near him. Alexander blinked nervously. 'You going to be a famous actress too?' Football asked him unkindly.

'He could easily get to be famous,' I said. 'He's dead brainy. Top of everything at school. He could go on all the quiz shows on the telly and know every single answer. Only you'd better have a special telly name. Alexander isn't exactly catchy. How about . . . Brainbox?'

I was trying to be nice to him but I didn't seem to have the knack. Alexander winced at the word.

'They call me that at school,' he said mournfully. 'And other stuff. And my dad calls me Mr Clever Dick.'

'He sounds a right charmer, your dad,' I said.

'*My* dad's the best *ever*,' said Football, kicking his ball from one foot to the other.

'I haven't got a dad so I don't know whether he's the best or the worst,' I said. I've never really fussed about it. I never needed a dad, not when I had a mum. I needed her.

'My mum's going to take me to live at her

place,' I told them. 'It's dead luxurious, all gilt and mirrors and chandeliers and rich ruby red upholstery. And she's going to buy me new clothes, designer stuff, and new trainers and a brand new computer and my own telly and a video and a bike and pets and we're going on heaps of trips to Disneyland and I bet we won't even have to queue because my mum's such a famous actress.'

'What's her name then?' Football demanded.

'Carly. Carly Beaker,' I said proudly.

'Never heard of her,' said Football.

I thought quickly. I had to shut him up somehow. 'That's not her acting name.'

'Which is?'

'Sharon Stone.'

'If your mum's Sharon Stone then my dad's Alan Shearer,' said Football.

Alexander's head jerked. 'Your dad's Alan Shearer?' he piped up. 'No wonder he's good at football.'

Football shook his head pityingly. 'I

thought he was supposed to be bright?' he said. 'Anyway, my dad's *better* than Alan Shearer. We're like *that*, my dad and me.' He linked his stubby fingers to show us. 'We do all sorts together. Well. We did.'

Significant past tense.

'He's got this girlfriend,' said Football. 'My mum found out and now my dad's gone off with this girlfriend. I don't blame him. My mum just nags and moans and gives him a hard time. No wonder he cleared off. But he says it doesn't mean we're not still mates.'

'So your dad doesn't live with you any more?' said Alexander, sighing enviously.

'But we still do all sorts of stuff together,' said Football, kicking the ball about again. 'We always go to the match on Saturdays. Well, Dad couldn't make it this time. And last time. But that's because he's still, like, sorting out his new life – he's taking me *next* time, he's promised.' He stepped on the ball and patted his pockets, bringing out a cigarette-lighter. 'Look!'

I looked. He didn't produce the packet of fags to go with it.

'Let's have a smoke then,' I said. I like the way my mum holds her hand when she's got a fag lit – and the way her lips purse as she takes a long drag.

'I don't smoke, it's bad for my football, right?' said Football. 'No, this is my dad's lighter. See the make?' He held it out so we could admire it. 'It's not one of your tacky throw-away sort. It's *gold*.'

'Solid gold!' Alexander whispered.

'Well. Plated. Still cost a fortune. It's my dad's most precious possession. His mates gave it to him for his twenty-first birthday. He's never without it, my dad.'

'He seems to be without it now,' I chipped in.

'That's the *point*,' said Football.
'He's given it to *me*.' He flicked it on and off, on and off, on and off. It was like watching those flashing Christmas tree lights.

'You'll be waving it around at a rock concert next,' I said.

'You shut your face,' said Football, irritated that I wasn't acting dead impressed. 'You haven't even got a dad.' He kicked the ball hard. It bounced on the television set and ended up inside it.

'I wish I didn't have a dad,' said Alexander,

standing up and attempting repairs. 'Or I wish my dad would go off with a girlfriend. I wish wishes would come true. What would you wish for?' He looked shyly at Football. 'That you and your dad could be together?'

'Yeah,' said Football, looking amazed that Alexander could possibly have sussed this out. '*And* to play for United,' he added.

'What about you, Tracy?' asked Alexander.

'I don't want a dad,' I said quickly.

'What about your mum?' Alexander persisted. 'Would you wish you and your mum could be together?'

'That would be a totally wasted wish, wouldn't it, because I'm going to be with her *anyway*.'

But I'll still wish it even so. Let me be with my mum. Let me be with my mum. I'm wishing with all my heart. And my lungs and my liver and my bones and my brains. All the strings of my intestines are tied in knots I'm wishing so hard.

Mum's Home

Wishes come true. My fairy godmother has been working overtime! She made it come true. I spent the whole weekend with my mum and it was WONDERFUL and she says she wants me to go and live with her for ever and ever and ever, just as soon as Elaine gets it all sorted out officially.

Elaine didn't think my mum would turn up. She didn't say anything, but I'm not daft. I could tell. Cam dumped me off at Elaine's office. She said she would wait with me if I wanted but I didn't want. It's kind of weird being with Cam at the moment. She's *still* not making a big fuss and begging me not to go. Though I heard her crying last night.

I heard these little muffled under-the-duvet

sobs – and I suddenly couldn't stand it and stumbled out of bed and went running across the hall. I was all set to jump into bed with Cam and give her a big hug and tell her . . .

Tell her *what*? That was the trouble. I couldn't tell her I wouldn't go because I've *got* to go. My mum's my *mum*. Cam isn't anybody. Not really. And I've known my mum all my life while I've only known Cam six months. You can't compare it, can you?

So I didn't go and give her a cuddle. I made out I needed a wee and went to the bathroom. When I padded back the sobs had stopped. Maybe I'd imagined them anyway.

I don't know why I'm going on about all this sad stuff when I'm HAPPY HAPPY HAPPY. My mum didn't let me down. She came for me at Elaine's.

She was a little bit late, so that I had to keep going to the toilet and Elaine's bottom lip started bleeding because she'd nibbled it so hard with her big bunny teeth – but then suddenly this taxi drew up outside and my mum got out and she came running in on her high heels, her

122

lovely blonde hair bouncing on her shoulders, her chest bouncing too in her tight jumper, and she clutched me tight in her arms so that I breathed her wonderful warm powdery smoky smell and then she said all this stuff about over-sleeping and missed trains and I didn't take any of it in, I was just so happy she was really there.

Though I didn't exactly *act* happy.

'Hey, hey, don't cry, kid, you're making my jumper all soggy,' Mum joked.

'I'm not crying. I never cry. I just get this hay fever sometimes, I told you,' I said, helping myself to Elaine's paper hankies.

Then Mum whisked me off and instead of bothering with boring old buses and trains we got into the taxi and drove all the way home. To Mum's house. Only it's going to be *my* house now.

It was miles and miles and miles and it cost a mega-fortune but do you know what my mum said? 'Never mind, darling, you're worth it!'

I very nearly had another attack of hay fever. And my mum didn't just fork out for the longest taxi ride in the world. Just wait till I write about all the presents! She's better than a fairy godmother! And her house is like a fairy palace too, even better than I ever imagined.

OK, it's not all that wonderful outside. Mum lives in this big block of flats on an estate and it's all car tyres and rubbish and scraggy kids outside. Mum's flat is right on the top floor and the lift swoops up faster than your stomach can cope. That's why I suddenly felt so weird – that and the pee smell in the lift. I got this feeling that the walls of the lift were pressing in on me, squashing me up so small I couldn't breathe. I wanted someone to come and hoick me out quick and tuck me up tight in my black bat cave. I didn't give so much as a squeak but Mum saw my face.

'Whatever's up with you, Tracy? You're not scared of a *lift*, are you? A big girl like you!'

She laughed at me and I tried to laugh too but it sounded more like I was crying. Only of course I don't ever cry. But it was all OK the minute I stepped *out* of the smelly old lift and *into* Mum's wonderful flat.

It's deep red – the carpet and the velvet curtains and the cushions, just as I'd hoped.

The sofa is white leather – s-o-o-o glamorous – and there's a white fur rug in front of it. The first thing Mum made me do was take my shoes off. I didn't notice the amazing twirly light fitting and the pictures of pretty ladies on the walls and the musical globe and the china figures at first because my eyes just got fixated on the sofa. Not because of the white leather. Because there was a pile of parcels in one corner, done up in pink paper with gold ribbon.

'Presents!' I breathed.

'That's right,' said Mum.

'Is it your birthday, Mum?'

'Of course it isn't, silly. They're for you!'

'It's not *my* birthday.'

'I know when your birthday is! I'm your *mum*. No, these are special presents for you because you're my own little girl.'

'Oh Mum!' I said – and I gave her this big hug. 'Oh Mum, oh Mum, oh Mum!'

'Come on then, don't you want to open them?'

'You bet I do!' I started tearing the paper off.

'Hey, hey, that cost ninety-nine pence a sheet. Careful!'

I went carefully, my hands trembling. I opened up the first parcel. It was a designer T-shirt, specially for me! I ripped off my own boring old one and squeezed into my BEAUTIFUL new status symbol.

'I could have got you a size or two bigger. I keep forgetting how big you are,' said Mum. 'Give it here, I'll change it for you.'

'No, no! It's wonderful! It's exactly the right size. Look, I can show my belly button and look dead sexy!' I did a little dance to demonstrate and Mum creased up laughing.

'You're a right little card, Tracy! Go on then, open the rest of your pressies.'

She gave me a fluffy pink rabbit. It's *lovely* if you like cuddly toys. Elaine would die for it. I decided to call it Marshmallow. I made it talk in a shy little lispy voice and Mum laughed again and said I was as good as any kid on the telly.

The next present was a H-U-G-E box of white chocolates. I ate two straight off, yum yum, slurp slurp. I wanted Mum to have one too but she said she was watching her figure, and they were all for me and I could eat as many as I liked. So I ate another two, yum yum, slurp slurp, same as before – but I started to feel a bit sickish again. They were WONDERFUL chocolates, and I bet they were mega-expensive, but somehow they weren't quite the same as Smarties. I know they'll be my favourites when I'm a bit older.

The last present wasn't for when I'm older. It was the biggest and Mum had left the price on the box so I knew it was most definitely the most expensive, amazingly so.

It was a doll. Not just any old doll, you understand. The most fantastic curly-haired Victorian doll in a flowery silk costume, with her own matching parasol clutched in her china hand.

I looked at her, holding the box.

'Well?' said Mum.

'Well. She's lovely. The loveliest doll in the whole world,' I said, trying to make my voice as bouncy as Football's ball, only it kind of rolled away from me and came out flat.

'You used to be such a dolly girl, even though you were a fierce little kid,' said Mum. 'Remember I bought you that wonderful big dolly with golden ringlets? You totally adored her. Wouldn't let her go. What did you call her? Rose, was it? Daffodil?'

'Bluebell.'

'So here's a sister for Bluebell.'

'That's great, Mum,' I said, my stomach squeezing.

'You've still got Bluebell, haven't you?' said Mum, squinting at me.

'Mmm,' I said. My tummy really hurt, as if this new doll had given it a hard poke with her pointy parasol.

'So did you bring her with you?' Mum persisted, lighting another cigarette.

'Give us a fag, Mum, go on, please,' I said, to try to divert her.

'Don't be so daft. You're not to start smoking, Tracy, it's a bad habit.' She started off this really Mumsie lecture and I dared breathe out. But my mum's not soft. 'So where *is* she then? Bluebell?' she persisted.

'I . . . I don't know,' I said. 'You see, the thing *is*, Mum, I had to leave her in the Children's Home.'

'They wouldn't let you take your own dolly?'

'She got a bit . . . broken.'

'You broke your doll?'

'No! No, it wasn't me, Mum, I swear it. It was one of the other kids. They poked her eyes out and cut off all her ringlets and scribbled on her face.'

'I don't *believe* it! That place! Well, I'll get on to Elaine the Pain straight away. That doll cost a fortune.'

'It happened years ago, Mum.'

'Years ago?' Mum shook her head. It was like she couldn't get her time scales right. She kept acting like she'd only popped me in the Children's Home last Tuesday when I've actually been in and out of care since I was little. My folder's *this* thick.

'Oh well,' said Mum. 'Anyway. You've got a new dolly now. Even better than Bluebell. What are you going to call this one? Not a daft name like Marshmallow this time. She's a beautiful doll. She needs a proper name.'

'I'll call her . . .' I tried hard but I couldn't come up with anything.

'What's your favourite name? You must have one,' said Mum.

'Camilla,' I said without thinking.

Mum stood still.

BIG MISTAKE.

'That woman's called Camilla, isn't she?' said Mum, drawing hard on her cigarette.

'No, no!' I gabbled. 'She's Cam. She never gets called Camilla. No, Mum, I like the name *Camilla* because there was this little girl in the Children's Home, *she* was called Camilla.'

I was telling the truth. I used to love this little kid Camilla, and she liked me too, she really did. I could always make her laugh. I just had to pull a funny face and blow a raspberry and Camilla would gurgle with laughter and clap her pudgy little hands.

Camilla's been my favourite name for ages, long long before I met Cam. Cam never gets called Camilla anyway. She can't stand it. She thinks it sounds all posh and pretentious. I tried hard to get Mum to believe me.

'Camilla,' Mum said, like it was some particularly smelly disease. 'Your favourite name, eh? Do you like it better than Carly?'

'Of course not,' I said. 'Carly's the best ever name, obviously, because it's yours. But I can't call the doll Carly because *you're* Carly. Hey, maybe she should be called Curly?' I scooped the doll out of her box and shook her so that her ringlets wiggled. 'Yeah, Curly!'

'Careful! You'll muck those eyes up too!' Mum took the doll from me and smoothed her satin skirts.

'It wasn't me that poked her eyes out.'

'Even so, you must play with her *gently*.' Mum handed her back to me.

I held her at arm's length, not quite sure what to do with her. 'Hello, Curly. Little girly Curly. Curlybonce!'

'That's not a very nice name. She's a very special collector's doll, Tracy. Don't you like her ringlets?'

'Yes, they're lovely.'

'It's about time we tried to do something with *your* hair. Come here.' She fiddled in her handbag and brought out a little hairbrush. 'Right!' She suddenly attacked my head.

'O-w-w-w-w-w!'

'Keep still!' said Mum, giving me a little tap with the brush.

'You're pulling my head off!'

'Nonsense. It seems like it hasn't been brushed for weeks. It's like a bird's nest.'

'O-u-c-h!'

'Do you make this fuss when Cam does your hair?'

'She doesn't.'

Mum sighed, shaking her head. 'I don't know, she's being paid a fortune, and yet she lets you wander round like a ragamuffin.'

'Cam's not really into how you look,' I said, trying really hard to hold my head still though it felt like she was raking grooves in my scalp.

'Typical,' said Mum. 'Well, *I* care how you look.'

'I care too, Mum,' I said. 'Ouch! No, it's OK, don't stop. We women have to suffer for our beauty, eh?'

Mum creased up laughing though I hadn't meant it as a joke. 'You're a funny little thing,' she said. She paused, tapping the back of her hairbrush on her palm. 'You do love me, don't you, darling?'

'*Ever* so much,' I shouted.

It still didn't sound loud enough to Mum. 'More than anyone else?'

'Yes!' I insisted, though my throat ached as I

said it. 'Yes. You bet. You're my mum.'

She reached out and patted my face, cupping my chin. 'And you're my little girl,' she said. 'Though you're getting to be such a big girl now.' She fingered my lips. 'They're all chapped. You need a spot of lip balm. Half a tick.' She rooted in her handbag amongst her make-up.

'Oh, Mum, make me up properly, eh?'

Mum put her head on one side, looking amused. 'It might help give you a bit more colour, I suppose.'

'Yeah, I want to look all colourful like you, Mum.'

She laughed. 'We've got different skin tones, pet. But I can certainly liven you up a bit. You've got quite a nice little face, though you must watch it when you scowl. You don't want to be all wrinkly when you're my age. *Smile*, Tracy.'

I smiled until my ears waggled.

'Maybe you could get away with a pale pink lipstick and a spot of rouge on your cheeks.'

'I want bright red lipstick like yours!' I had a rootle in her bag myself.

'Get out of there!' said Mum, trying to snatch it back. 'Tracy! You're mucking up all my things.'

I'd found a red mock-crocodile wallet.

'You after my money?' said Mum.

'Is there a photo of me inside?' I said, opening it.

I peered. There *was* a photo but it certainly wasn't me. 'Who's he?' I asked.

'Give that wallet here,' said Mum, acting like she meant it now.

'Who's the guy?' I asked, handing it over.

'He's no-one,' said Mum. She took the photo out of the plastic frame. 'This is what I think of *him*,' she said, and she tore the photo into tiny little bits.

'Is it my dad?'

'No!' said Mum, sounding amazed, like she'd forgotten I'd ever had a dad. 'No, it's my boyfriend. My ex.'

'The one that went off with the young girl?'

'That's the one,' said Mum. 'The *slug*. Still, who needs him, that's what I say.'

I said he'd have to be crazy to go off with anyone else when he had someone as beautiful as Mum. She liked this a lot. We sat down on the sofa together, and I put Curly carefully on my lap and tucked Marshmallow under my arm. Mum fed me another white chocolate. I didn't really fancy it but I ate it up anyway, licking her long pointy fingers so that she squealed.

'You and me will be all right, won't we, Tracy?' said Mum. It seemed like she was seriously asking me.

'We're going to be just great,' I said.

'We'll stay together, yes?'

'Yes, yes, yes!'

'It's what you want?' Mum persisted.

'More than anything in the world,' I said.

We had a huge hug, Mum and me (Curly and Marshmallow got a bit squashed but Mum didn't nag), and it was like we were spinning in our *own* little world, and it was whirling us all the way up into outer space.

The Tree Home

I got a bit miffed when I went back to my home. Football and Alexander were there already, playing football. Well, Football did the kicking. Maybe Alexander was meant to be the goalie. He seemed to be acting as a goalpost too.

I didn't think they had any right to be there. Well, not before me. I flounced back to the kitchen. Alexander had supplied the cardboard refrigerator with a packet of Jaffa Cakes. I felt this was extra mean as I'm not very keen on orange. I ate three even so, just to show him. I wanted a drink but there was just this silly cardboard cut-out kettle. I scrumpled it up. What sort of idiot was he?

'It took me a long time to get the sides equal and the spout right,' Alexander said reproachfully, standing in the kitchen doorway.

'Never mind your silly bits of cardboard!

Hey, you'll never ever guess what!'

'What?' said Alexander.

'I'm going to live with my mum.'

'Are you?' said Alexander, as if I'd said 'I'm going to help myself to another Jaffa Cake'.

'What do you *mean* "are you"? That's a bit of a limpy wimpy response. Why aren't you, like, "Wow, Tracy, you lucky thing, how fantastic, super-duper mega-whizzo brilliant"?'

Alexander stood to attention. 'Wow, Tracy. You lucky thing,' he said obediently. Then he paused. 'What else was it?' He was acting like he didn't think I was the luckiest kid in the whole world.

'Look, you haven't *seen* my mum.' I wished I had a photo to show him. 'She looks totally fantastic. She's really really beautiful, and she wears these wonderful clothes, and her hair and her make-up are perfect. She made me up too and styled my hair and I looked incredible.'

There was a very rude snort from the living room where Football was obviously flapping his ears, listening to every word.

I marched in to confront him, Alexander shuffling after me. Football dodged back and shielded his face, pretending to be dazzled. 'Here's Tracy the Incredible Beauty!' he said, fooling about.

I gave him an extra withering look. 'You can scoff all you like, but maybe I'll take after my mum and end up looking just like her,' I said.

'And maybe that's a little fat piggy flying through the air,' said Football.

Alexander's head turned, mouth open, looking for the flying pig.

'My mum's given me all these presents too,' I said. 'Heaps and heaps.'

'Whoops! There's a whole herd of piggies flying past,' said Football.

Alexander blinked and then got it at last and chortled loudly.

'It's true! She's spent a fortune on me. She's given me everything I could ever want.'

'What, the computer? And the rollerblades and the mountain bike?' said Football, starting to look impressed at long last.

I hesitated. 'She's giving me all those later, when I'm living with her.'

'Aha!' said Football.

'But she's already given me this new T-shirt. Look, it's designer, none of your market copy rubbish either, look at the label.'

'Cool,' said Football.

'*And* she gave me this enormous box of chocolates, so many I couldn't possibly eat them all.'

'Well, maybe you could pop them in our fridge,' said Alexander, still giggling weakly. 'We're a bit short on provisions at the moment.'

'Yeah, well, they're fresh cream, and when I got them back to Cam's they'd gone a bit funny-tasting so we had to throw them out. But I've still got the box. I'll show you it if you don't believe me, Football. And my mum gave me heaps of other stuff too, the most fantastic cuddly toys and a special collector's doll, an actual modern antique that costs hundreds of pounds.'

'A doll?' said Football.

'Well, it's more like a giant ornament. I tell you, it's simply beautiful. My mum's the greatest mum in all the world.'

Alexander was looking serious again, his eyes beady.

'What?' I said.

'She can't really be the best mum, not if she left you,' he said. 'I think if you leave your little girl it makes you a bad mum.'

'She couldn't help it,' I said quickly. 'It was just the way things were. She had things to do. And she had this really gross boyfriend. She didn't have any option. She thought I'd be fine in the Children's Home.'

'I thought you hated it,' said Alexander. He was really starting to get on my nerves.

'I got along OK,' I said fiercely.

'Not till Cam came along,' Alexander persisted. 'What about Cam, Tracy?'

'What about her?' I said, sticking my face into his and baring my teeth. I was very nearly tempted to bite. 'My mum says she can't really care about me. She's just fostering me for the money.'

'You can't be *easy* to foster, Tracy,' said Alexander, backing away from me. But he still wouldn't shut up. 'I think she's fostering you because she likes you. Don't you like her?'

141

'She's all right,' I said awkwardly. 'Anyway she can't like me all that much or she'd fight harder to keep me, wouldn't she?'

Alexander deliberated. 'Maybe she's just trying to fit in with what *you* want because she likes you lots and lots.'

'Maybe you should just shut up and mind your own business,' I said. 'What do you know anyway, Alexander-the-totally-teeny-tiny-gherkin.'

I gave him a push and waved at Football. 'Come on, let's play footie then. I'll give you a *real* game.'

Football stopped staring and sprang into action. He passed the ball to me and I kicked it so hard it bounced back off the opposite wall, hit the sofa, and then ricocheted straight into the television set.

'That's the second television gone for a burton – and it takes ages to make,' Alexander wailed.

'You and your stupid cardboard rubbish. Let's clear it all out the way,' I said, giving the crumpled cardboard another kick for good measure.

Alexander looked as if he was about to cry. I don't know why. I wasn't kicking *him*. But when Football caught on and got ready for a major WRECK-THE-JOINT I diverted him upstairs where it wouldn't matter so much. Alexander hadn't attempted any Interior Design – but there were old boxes to kick to bits and a filthy old mattress to jump on.

Alexander came trailing upstairs after us and stood anxiously in the doorway, not daring to join in. I felt mean, but I still couldn't forgive him for being so obstinate about my mum.

Football went into Major Demolition Mode for a minute or two and then decided to take a rest.

'You think it's great I'm going to live with my mum, don't you, Football?' I said. 'Hey, don't *lie* on the mattress, you'll get fleas.'

'Yuck!' said Football, leaping up again. 'Yeah, I think it's good about your mum, seeing as she's going to be giving you all them presents. You've got to look out for number one, Tracy. Go for what you can get and the one who'll give you the most.' He kicked his ball against the wall and then jumped up and headed it expertly back again. 'Wow! Did you see that?' He waved his arms in the air, showing off like mad.

'It's not just the presents and stuff,' I said. 'It's because she's my *mum*.'

'Mums are rubbish,' said Football.

'You wouldn't say that about dads!'

'Yes I would,' said Football, and this time he kicked the ball so dementedly it veered off the wall and smashed the opposite window. It disappeared out of sight.

'Whoops!' said Football.

'I think maybe that's enough wrecking,' I said.

'Watch that broken glass, Football,' said Alexander. 'You'll cut yourself.'

'What are you doing, you nutter?' I said, as Football opened the window, spraying more glass all over the place.

'We need a dustpan and brush,' said Alexander. 'Maybe I can devise something out of cardboard?'

'You and your daft bits of cardboard,' I said. 'Hey, Football, what are you doing *now*?'

Football was climbing out of the window!

'I'm getting my ball back,' said

Football, peering out. 'It hasn't come down. It's stuck up on the guttering, look!'

'Football, get back!'

'It's terribly dangerous, Football!'

'Not the drainpipe!'

'You're far too big. Don't!'

Football did. He reached for the drainpipe. It wobbled and then started to buckle. Football let go sharpish.

'Get back *in*, Football,' I said, clawing at his ankles.

He kicked my hands hard – and then leapt.

I screamed and shut my eyes. I waited for the crash and thump. But there wasn't one.

Alexander was making little gaspy noises beside me. 'Look at him!' he whispered.

I opened my eyes and stared in disbelief. Football had leapt across a sickening gap into the fir tree that grew up against the wall. He made loud triumphant Tarzan noises.

'You're *crazy*!'

'No, I'm not! Haven't you ever climbed a tree? And this one's a piece of cake, just like going up a ladder.'

Football climbed up steadily while we craned our necks, watching. Alexander gripped my hand tight, his sharp little nails digging into my palm.

Football very nearly reached the top, reached out – and clawed his ball back from the guttering. 'Yuck, it's got gunge all over it,' he said, wiping it on the tree branches.

'Just come back down, you nutter!' I yelled.

'I'll wash it for you, Football,' Alexander offered. 'Please, just come back!'

So Football climbed down again, threw the ball back in the broken window, leant over the dizzying drop, leapt for it, teetered on the window ledge, and then came crashing into the bedroom on top of us.

For a moment we were all too stunned to say anything. Football got up first. Alexander and I didn't have any option, seeing as he was on top of us.

'Dads *are* rubbish,' Football said, dusting himself down and wiping the gungy ball on Alexander's jersey. 'Smelly mouldering putrid rubbish.'

It was like there'd been no break in the conversation whatsoever.

'But you're nuts about your dad,' I said, getting up gingerly and waggling my arms and legs to make sure they weren't broken.

'That's what I was. Nuts,' said Football. 'That's your new nickname for me, isn't it? Nutter?'

Alexander sat up and looked at his stained jumper. 'It's my school one,' he said, in a very little voice. Then he swallowed hard. 'Still, it doesn't really matter, seeing as I hardly ever go to school now.'

'Oh dear, have I spoilt your school jersey?' said Football. 'I'm terribly sorry, Alexander, old chum.'

Alexander chose to take him seriously. 'That's quite all right, Football,' he said. He got up cautiously as if there was every chance he might be knocked down again. 'What happened with your dad, Football?'

I held my breath.

'You shut up, useless,' said Football, but he simply bounced his ball on Alexander's head.

'Didn't your dad take you to the match on Saturday?' I asked.

Football suddenly sat back down himself,

his back against the wall. He looked down at the bare floorboards. He didn't even bounce his ball. 'I waited. And waited. And waited,' he mumbled. 'But he never turned up.'

Football thought there was something wrong, like his dad was ill or in trouble, so he went round to his place, only there was no-one there. He sat on the steps outside his flat and waited for ages. Then when his dad eventually turned up he had his girlfriend with him, and he was slobbering all over her like she was an ice lolly. Football looked like he was going to be sick when he told us. And it got worse.

It turned out his dad had taken the girlfriend to the match instead of Football because she'd got this thing about the goalie's *legs*. They both laughed like it was really cute and funny and had no idea what they were doing to Football. He made out he didn't care. He said he was getting a bit sick of their football Saturdays anyway. And his dad got shirty then and said, Right, if that's your attitude . . .

So Football pushed off and then when he

got back home his mum saw he was upset but it just made her mad and she slagged off his dad all over again.

'So I called her all these names and said it was no wonder Dad left home because she's such a whining misery. Then she clumped me and cried and now she's not talking to me. So they both hate me, my mum and my dad. So they're rubbish, right? All mums and dads are rubbish.'

He stopped. We seemed to have stopped too. The house was very quiet. It was chilly with the window broken. I shivered.

'It doesn't necessarily follow that *all* mums and dads are rubbish,' said Alexander.

There are some silences that shouldn't be broken. Football bounced his ball at Alexander's head again. Hard.

'I don't really like it when you do that, Football,' Alexander said, blinking.

'Good,' said Football. He bounced his ball again. It was unfortunate for Alexander that Football has deadly accurate aim.

'Tracy?' Alexander said, a tear rolling down his cheek.

I felt like there were two Tracys.

One wanted to put her arm round him and wipe his eyes and yell at Football to go and pick on someone his own size. And the other wanted to bounce a ball on his brainy little bonce too.

The Tracy twins argued it out. Guess which one won.

'You're such a wimp, Alexander. Why can't you stick up for yourself? You daren't do anything.'

Alexander drooped. 'I *did* do that dare,' he said. 'Even though it meant the whole school called me names.'

'What dare?' said Football, still bouncing.

'I'm Tracy Beaker, the Great Inventor of Extremely Outrageous Dares,' I said proudly.

'Like?' said Football, catching the ball.

'Like anything,' I said.

'So dare me,' said Football, swaggering.

I let half a dozen ideas flicker in my head. None of them seemed quite suitable for Football. I squeezed my brain hard. I needed something suitably scary, rude and revolting.

Alexander seemed to think I needed help. 'Tracy dared wave her knickers in the air!' he announced.

'Shut *up*, Alexander!' I hissed.

Football grinned. 'OK, Tracy, I dare you wave your knickers. Go on!'

'Get lost,' I said. 'And anyway, you can't copy my dare.'

'All right. I'll think of a better one.' Football was grinning from ear to ear now. 'I dare you take your knickers off and hang them on the fir tree like a Christmas decoration!'

I stared at him. It wasn't fair. It was a BRILLIANT dare. Definitely Tracy Beaker standard. Oh how I wanted to zip his grin up!

'You can't ask Tracy to do that!' said Alexander. 'It's far too dangerous.'

'*I* climbed out into the tree,' said Football.

'Yes, but you're bigger and stronger than Tracy,' said Alexander. 'And madder,' he added softly.

'There isn't anyone madder than me,' I said. 'OK, I'll do your stupid old dare, Football, easy-peasy.'

'Tracy!' said Alexander. He looked at me, he looked at Football. 'Is this just a game?'

'It's *my* game, my Dare Game,' I said. 'Only it's way too daring for you, Little Gherkin.'

'Gherkin?' said Football. 'One of them

151

little wizened pickled things?'

'Alexander gets called Gherkin because everyone's seen what he looks like in the showers!'

Football cracked up laughing. 'Gherkin! That's a good one! *Gherkin!*'

Alexander looked at me, his eyes huge in his pinched face. 'Why are you being so mean to me today, Tracy?'

'*You're* mean to me, trying to stop me living happily ever after with my mum, when it's what I've always wanted more than anything in the whole world,' I said, and I marched to the window, kicking the broken glass out the way, and hitched myself up onto the window ledge.

'Tracy! Don't! What if you fall?' Alexander shrieked.

I hooked one leg out.

'Tracy! I wasn't serious. You're too little,' Football shouted.

'I'm not little! I'm Tracy the Great and I always win every single dare,' I yelled, getting the other leg out and standing up straight. Straightish. My legs were a bit wobbly.

I looked down – and then wished I hadn't.

'Come back, Tracy!' said Alexander.

But I couldn't go back. I had to go forward. 'This is the Dare Game, and I'm going to win it, just you wait and see.'

I looked at the tree – and jumped. One second I was in the air and there were screams – some mine – and then I had twigs up my nose and scratching my face and I was clinging there, in the tree, hands hanging onto branches, feet curled against the trunk.

I'd made it! I hadn't fallen! I had managed a thrilling death-defying l-e-a-p! Football gave his Tarzan cry behind me and I joined in too, long and loud.

'Now come back in, Tracy,' Alexander pleaded.

'I haven't started yet!' I said. 'Shut your eyes. And you, Football.'

They both blinked at me like they'd forgotten the whole point of the dare.

'I've got to take my knickers off now, so *no* peeping,' I commanded.

They shut their eyes obediently. Well, one of them did.

'Football! Think I'm daft? Stop squinting at me!' I yelled.

Football's eyes shut properly this time. I gingerly let go of the branch and started  fidgeting under my skirt. It was a lot more scary only holding on with one hand. It would have been much more sensible to take my knickers off *before* I was in the tree, but it was too late now. I got them around my knees, and then reached down. The garden wavered way down below me and I felt sick.

'Don't, Tracy! You'll fall!' Football shouted.

'Shut your ****** eyes!' I was so peeved he was peering right up my short skirt I forgot to be frightened, eased my knickers over my foot and then straightened up in a flash.

'They're off!' I yelled, waving them like a flag.

Football cheered. 'Shove them on a branch for a second and then get back in,' he shouted. 'You've won the bet, Trace. Good for you.'

'Yes, come back *now*, Tracy,' said Alexander.

I didn't want to come back right that instant.

I was starting to get used to it in the tree. I looked up instead of down. It was a great feeling to be up so high. I reached for the next branch and the next and the next.

The boys yelled at me but I took no notice. I'd turned into Monkey Girl, leaping about the treetops without a worry in the world.

The tree swayed a little more as I got nearer the top, but I didn't mind a bit. It felt soothing, not scary. If I was Monkey Girl I could swing in my tree all day long and at night I could fashion myself a leafy hammock and rock myself to sleep.

I started to think seriously about a tree-house. I could get Alexander to design it – *not* one of his cardboard concoctions, a proper planks of wood job. Football and I could knock it together and somehow secure it to the tree. Yes, a treehouse would be absolutely amazing. I could furnish it with blankets and cushions and have heaps of provisions and I could live up there all the time and spy on all my enemies and everyone would talk in awed tones about Tracy of the Treetops.

I decided to make a start on the treehouse idea for real, but then I remembered I was going to live with my mum any minute now so there wasn't any point and I got a bit distracted – and slipped. I scrabbled and grabbed the next branch down, hanging on for dear life. Or lousy life. Any kind of life.

'Watch out, Tracy!'

'Tracy! Come back! *You're* the nutter now!'

My heart was hammering and my hands were slippy with sweat but I thought I'd wind them up just a little bit more. I climbed higher, up and up, branch after branch, hand over hand, foot after foot, concentrating fiercely now. I climbed until I was fast running out of tree, the branches becoming so delicate and spindly that some broke right off when I took hold of them – but I dared go even higher so that I could just about reach up up up to the very top. I hooked my knickers round and attached them to the tip like a big white star.

I saw stars too, a whole galaxy of constellations shining and sparkling in celebration. I'd done it! The most Daring Dare ever and *I'd done it.*

Then I climbed all the way down, feeling my way with my feet, down and down and down until at long last I came level with the window, and there were Football and Alexander gazing out at me open-mouthed as if I was an angel swooping straight down from heaven.

'Out the way then, you gawpers,' I commanded, and they drew apart like curtains.

I got ready to spring.

I made it right through the window. I didn't even fall over. I landed on my feet. Tracy the Fabulous Cat Girl with all her nine lives still in front of her.

'How about *that*!' I said, and I did this crazy dance around the room.

Football danced with me, leaping about, clapping me on the back. 'You're the greatest, kid. Knickers off and all!'

'Yeah, I'm the greatest, aren't I? Aren't I, Alexander?'

'You're the maddest!' said Alexander. 'I'm a total jelly with watching you. Look, I'm still shaking.'

'Gherkin jelly! Yuck,' I said.

'You're mad. You're both mad,' said Alexander. 'Can't you see? You could have been killed. It *doesn't* make you the greatest.'

'No, *you're* the greatest! The greatest meanest bore ever,' I said, poking him. How dare he try to spoil my Stupendous Achievement?

'She *is* the greatest. And so am I,' said Football, poking him too.

'Stop poking me,' said Alexander, hunching up small. 'You're not not not great, not just because you take stupid risks and nearly kill yourselves.'

I was starting to feel like killing Alexander. He was acting like this irritating little gnat nipping away at my ankles. Any second now I'd stick out my hand and go SWAT.

'Don't make me really mad, Alexander,' I warned him, giving him another poke.

'You're already mad at me for saying all that stuff about your mum. That's why you keep picking on me.'

'That's got nothing to do with it,' I said fiercely. I'm mad at you because you're *maddening*!'

'No wonder they all pick on you at your school,' Football jeered. 'No wonder even your own dad can't stand you.' He didn't touch him this time but somehow it was worse than a poke.

I wavered just a weeny bit. 'Well, he must like him really.'

'No he doesn't,' said Alexander. Big tears were rolling down his cheeks. 'He can't stand me.'

I felt so mean that it made me even angrier with him. 'That's rubbish! Don't be so stupid.' I gave him a sudden push. 'You're *really* starting to irritate me now.'

'You've always irritated me, Gherkin,' said Football.

'Don't call me that,' Alexander said, sniffling.

'Gherkin, Gherkin, Gherkin!' Football chanted. 'Wizened little Gherkin who can't play the Dare Game.'

'I *did* play it! I did do a dare, didn't I, Tracy?'

'Yeah, you were mad enough to tell the whole school to call you Gherkin!'

'Stop it!'

'Gherkin, Gherkin, Gherkin!' I yelled, right in his face.

Football was right beside me. 'You clear off, Gherkin, this is *our* house,' he said.

'I was here first,' Alexander wept.

'But we're here now,' I said.

'And we don't want you, do we, Trace?'

I couldn't be quite that mean. There was still a bit of me that wanted to put my arms round Alexander and give him a hug.

Alexander saw me wavering. He gave a giant sniff. 'I'll do another dare if you let me stay!'

'OK then, climb up the tree and fetch

160

Tracy's knickers back,' said Football, quick as a wink.

'No!' I said.

'Yes!' said Football.

'All right,' said Alexander.

'Don't be crazy,' I said, suddenly scared. It was like everything was spinning too fast and I couldn't stop it. 'Football, please. You can't dare him to do that.'

'*I* did it,' said Football. 'And you did it too, even though you're little and only a girl.'

'*I'll* do it,' said Alexander. 'I still think it's mad and I'll probably get killed but I don't care. I'll still do it. I'll show you.' He ran to the window.

'You mustn't, Alexander!' I ran after him, but he was surprisingly fast. 'You can't climb, you can't balance, you can't do anything! You'll fall!'

'I told you, I don't care,' said Alexander, and he tried to jump up on the window ledge. He mistimed it completely and banged his nose hard on the window frame.

'See, Alexander! Now you're the one who's being stupid,' I said, rushing to him.

He shook his head, stunned, his nose crimson.

'Football, take the dare back quick,' I said.

'OK, OK, I take the dare back, Gherkin,' said Football.

'I'll still do the dare if you promise never ever to call me Gherkin again,' said Alexander, his voice muffled because his hands were cupping his sore nose.

'You're not doing any dare. You're right, we were all crazy.'

'You told me to go away,' said Alexander, turning to the window.

'I didn't mean it,' I said. 'You're my friend, Alexander. I like you. Football likes you too.'

'No I don't,' said Football.

'You *do*!' I insisted.

'No-one likes me, not really,' said Alexander, and he made another dash for the

window, a sudden quick dart that took us by surprise.

He jumped high enough this time. He made the window ledge. But he didn't stop. He swooped right out into space, like a little cartoon animal running in mid-air. But

Alexander was real. He didn't hang, give a yelp, and pedal backwards. He plummeted down . . . down down down into the dark garden below.

The Garden Home

We thought he was dead. He was still lying motionless when we hurtled downstairs and out the back window into the overgrown garden, his skinny arms and legs spread wide.

'Alexander!' I cried.

'He's copped it,' said Football – and he started to snuffle. 'I've murdered poor little Gherkin.'

'You're never to call me Gherkin again,' Alexander squeaked in a little mouse voice.

We fell on him, hugging him like he was our dearest friend.

'Careful!' said Alexander. 'I've probably broken my neck. And my arms and legs. And all my ribs.'

'Does it hurt terribly?' I said, taking his little claw hand in mine.

'I'm not sure,' said Alexander. 'I feel weird, like I can't feel anything properly yet. But I think it might hurt a lot when I can.'

'What do you mean, you can't feel anything? Oh no, he's paralysed!' said Football.

I tickled the backs of Alexander's knees and he squealed and kicked. 'No he's not,' I said.

Do you know the most amazing thing ever????

Alexander wasn't hurt at all. He didn't break so much as a fingernail! We stared at him in awe, wondering how he could possibly have survived that great drop unscathed. I'd always thought there was something not quite human about Alexander. Perhaps he was really an alien from another planet? That would explain a lot.

But the real reason for Alexander's remarkable survival only became apparent when he very gingerly got onto all fours and then stood up. He had fallen onto an old discarded mattress!

'You must be the luckiest kid ever!' I said.

'Though you might have a fleabite or two,' said Football.

'I think I *might* have hurt myself somewhere,' said Alexander, sounding wistful. 'This leg feels a bit odd. It's throbbing. I think I could have broken it. Definitely.'

'You couldn't possibly have broken your leg,' said Football. 'You'd be, like . . .' He mimed a footballer writhing on his back. 'You'd have to be stretchered off.'

'Maybe . . . maybe I'm just better at putting up with the pain,' said Alexander, experimenting with a limp.

'It was your *other* leg you were rubbing a minute ago.'

'Perhaps I've broken both,' Alexander persisted.

'You haven't broken anything at all and I'm so *glad*, Alexander,' I said, giving him another hug.

'Yeah, me too,' Football said gruffly.

'And you won't call me the G word ever again?'

'Right.'

'Because I did almost do the dare, didn't I?' said Alexander. 'Maybe I *am* Alexander the Great.'

'You're Alexander the Small,' said Football, patting him.

'You're Football the ever so Tall,' said Alexander. He turned to me. 'And you're Trace who wins every race. OK?'

'OK.'

'And we're all friends now?' said Alexander.

'Yes, of course we are,' I said. 'Alexander, stop limping. There's nothing the matter with your leg.'

'There is,' said Alexander. 'If I've got a broken leg I won't have to do PE at school.'

'You're never at school anyway,' I said.

'No, but I might have to be soon,' said Alexander, sighing. 'They wrote a letter to my mum and dad and they went nuts. My dad says he's going to escort me to school himself.'

'You're going to enjoy that!' I said.

'So it's just going to be you and me hanging out at the house, Tracy?' said Football.

'Well. I can't, can I? Not if I'm at my mum's. I'll be moving right away. Hey, my mum's flat is incredible, you should see all the stuff she's got!'

They didn't seem that interested. 'You'll just muck it all up anyway,' said Football.

'No I won't!'

I've got it all sussed out. I'm going to dust all her dinky little ornaments and vacuum the carpets and Mum will think I'm s-o-o-o useful she'll never ever get fed up with me and send me away again.

'I'm going to be my mum's little treasure,' I declared.

'I don't know why you want to go and stay with her,' said Football. 'You must be mad. She *is* mad, isn't she, Gherkin?'

'You're not to call me that!' Alexander said, stamping his foot. 'Ouch! That was my bad leg.'

'Sorry, sorry! But she *is* mad, isn't she?' said Football.

Alexander glanced at me nervously – but nodded.

'Who cares what you two think?' I said fiercely.

They were wrong. I wasn't mad. Any girl would want to live with her mum. Even a girl who already had a sort-of mum.

I haven't written much about Cam recently. There have been lots and lots of Cam bits. I just haven't felt like writing them. I mean, writers can't put *everything* down. If you started writing everything exactly as it happened you'd end up with page after page about opening your eyes and snuggling down in bed for another five minutes and then getting up and going to the loo and brushing your teeth and playing games squeezing your name out in paste and seeing what you'd look like with a toothbrush moustache . . . well, you'd need a whole new chapter before you'd even got started on breakfast.

Writers have to be selective. That's what Mrs Vomit Bagley says. Did I put that she's got wondrously unfortunate teeth? She spits a little bit whenever she says an 's' word. If

she's standing too near you then you're *not* wondrously fortunate because you get a little spray of V.B. saliva all over your face. Not that this has happened to me recently as I've hardly been to school, I've just been bunking off to go to the house.

They'll be getting in touch with Cam any minute. Maybe it's just as well I'm going off to my mum's. No, it's weller than well. I can't wait. I wish it wasn't being done in all these daft stages. Elaine says I can go for a week. I can't see why I can't go for ever right away. All this packing and unpacking is starting to get on my nerves.

Cam said she'd help me pack, but then she kept saying I didn't need this and I didn't need that – and *I* said it would be sensible to take nearly all my stuff seeing as I'd be staying there permanently soon.

Permanently was a very dramatic sort of word. It was like it bounced backwards and forwards between us long after I'd said it. As if it was knocking us both on the head.

Then Cam blinked hard and said, 'Right, yes, of course, OK,' in a quick gabble, shoving all my stuff in a suitcase, while *I* said, 'Perhaps it's a bit daft, and anyway, my mum will probably buy me all sorts of new stuff. Designer. Calvin Klein, Tommy Hilfiger—'

'NYDK, yes, yes, you keep saying.'

'DKNY! Honestly, you don't know anything, Cam,' I said, exasperated.

'I know one thing,' said Cam quietly. 'I'm going to miss you, kid.'

I swallowed hard. 'Well, I'll miss you too. I expect.' I hated the way she was looking at me. It wasn't *fair*. 'Fostering isn't, like, permanent,' I said. 'They told you that right at the beginning, didn't they?'

'They told me,' said Cam. She picked up one of my old T-shirts and hung onto it like it was a cuddle blanket. 'But I didn't get what it would feel like.'

'I'm sorry, Cam,' I said. 'I am. Really. But I've got to be with my mum.'

'I know,' said Cam. She hesitated. She looked down at the T-shirt as if I was inside it. 'But Tracy . . . don't get too upset if it doesn't quite work out the way you want.'

'It *is* working out!'

'I know, I know. And it's great that you're being reunited with your mum, but maybe you'll find it won't end up like a fairy story, happy ever after, for ever and ever.'

It will, it will. She just doesn't want it to.

'It *will* end happily ever after, you wait and see,' I said, pulling my T-shirt away from her and stuffing it in my suitcase with all the others.

'Tracy, I know—'

'You don't know anything!' I interrupted. 'You don't know my mum. You don't even know *me* properly. It's not like we've been together ages and ages. I don't see why you have to be

172

so . . . so . . . so shaking your head and giving me all these little warnings about it not working out. You obviously think I'm so horrible and bad and difficult that my mum will get sick of me in two seconds.'

'I don't think that at *all*. And you're *not* horrible and bad and difficult. Well, you *are* – but you can be great too. It's just that even if you're the greatest kid in the whole world and behave beautifully with your mum it *still* might not work out. Your mum isn't used to kids.'

'Neither were you, but you took me on.' Ah! I had a sudden idea. 'You can take some other kid now.'

'I don't want some other kid,' said Cam. She put her arm round me. 'I want you.'

I could hardly breathe. I wanted to cuddle close and hang onto her and tell her . . . tell her all sorts of stupid things. But I *also* wanted to shove her hard and shout at her for spoiling my big chance to get back to my mum.

I wriggled away from her and went on packing my suitcase. 'If you *really* wanted me you'd have made far more fuss in the first place,' I said, tucking my scrubby old trainers under my gungy chainstore denims. 'You'd have bought me decent clothes. And proper presents.'

'Oh Tracy, don't start,' said Cam, suddenly cross. She got up and started marching round my bat cave in an agitated fashion like she was a dog with fleas.

'You've hardly given me anything,' I said, cross too. 'I've never known anyone so stingy. And yet look at all the stuff my mum's given me.'

'A doll,' said Cam, picking it up. She held it at arm's length.

'Yes, but it's not like it's any old doll. It cost a fortune. It's not a little kid's doll, it's a collector's item. She gave it me like an ornament. Lots of grown-up ladies have doll collections. You wouldn't understand.' I sneered at Cam in her worn old plaid shirt and baggy jeans. 'You're not that sort of lady.'

'Thank God,' said Cam.

'I don't fit in here, Cam. Not with you. Or Jane and Liz and all your other stupid friends. I fit with my mum. Her and me. We're relatives. You're just my foster mum. You just get paid to look after me, that's all. I bet that's why you're making all the fuss, because you'll miss the cash when I'm gone.'

'Think that if you want, Tracy,' said Cam in this irritating martyr voice.

'It's true!'

'OK, OK,' said Cam, folding her arms.

'It *isn't* OK!' I said, stamping my foot. 'I don't know what you do with the money. It isn't like you spend it on me.'

'That's right,' said Cam, in this maddening there-there-I'll-agree-with-whatever-you-say-you-stupid-fool voice.

'It's *wrong* – and I'm sick of it,' I shouted. 'Do you know something? Even if it doesn't work out with my mum I still don't want to come back here. I'm sick of this boring old dump. I'm sick of you.'

'Well clear off then, you ungrateful little beast. I'm sick of you too!' Cam yelled, and she banged out of the bat cave in tears.

There. That's what she thinks of me. Well, see if I care. UNGRATEFUL. Why do I always have to be *grateful* to people?

Kids are always expected to be grateful grateful grateful. It's hateful being grateful. It's not fair. I'm supposed to be grateful to Cam for looking after me but I'm not allowed to look after myself. Though I could, easy-peasy. I'm supposed to be grateful for my yucky veggie meals (she hardly *ever* takes me to McDonald's) and my unstylish chainstore clothes (no wonder they pick on me at school) and my boring old books (honestly, have you *tried* reading *Little Women*? – who cares if Jo was Cam's all-time favourite book character?) and trips to museums (OK, I liked seeing the mummies and the little hunched-up dead man but all those pictures and pots were the *pits*).

If I could only earn my own money I could buy all the stuff I really need. It's not fair that kids aren't allowed to work. I'd be great flogging stuff down the market or selling ice creams or working in a nursery. If I could only get a job I could eat Big Macs and french fries every day and wear designer from top to toe, yeah, especially my footware, and buy all the videos and computer games I want and take a trip to Disneyland.

Yeah! I bet my mum will take me to Disneyland if I ask her.

It *is* going to end up like a fairy story. I'm going to live happily ever after.

I am.

Even if Football doesn't think so. I hate him.

No I don't. I quite like him in a weird sort of way. I'm worried about him. *He's* not going to live happily ever after.

I went to our house to say goodbye to Football and Alexander, seeing as I'm going to my mum's.

Alexander wasn't there. I didn't think Football was either. I went into the house and there was no sign of anyone – and no provisions in the cardboard fridge either. I checked upstairs and looked out of the window at the tree. My knickers were still up there. The tree seemed a long way from the window. We were all crazy. I looked down, my heart thudding when I thought of Alexander. And then I screamed.

Someone was lying spread-eagled on the mattress. Someone bigger than Alexander. Someone wearing last year's football strip.

'Football!' I yelled, and hurtled back inside the house and out the back window and down the overgrown garden to the mattress. 'Football, Football, Football!' I cried, standing over his still sprawled body.

He opened his eyes and peered at me. 'Tracy?'

'Oh, Football, you're alive!' I cried, going down on my knees beside him.

'Ooh Tracy, I didn't know you cared,' he said, giggling.

I gave him a quick flick round the face. 'Quit that, idiot! Did you fall?'

'I'm just having a little lie down.'

I touched his arm. He was icy cold and his shirt was damp. 'Have you been here all *night*? You're crazy.'

'Yeah. That's me. Mad. Nuts. Totally out of it.'

'You are,' I said. 'You'll make yourself ill.'

'So what?'

'You won't be able to play football.'

'Sure I will.' He reached for his football at the edge of the mattress and threw it in the air. He tried to catch it but it bounced off his finger-tips into the undergrowth.

Football swore, but didn't bother to get up. He lay where he was, flicking his dad's lighter on and off, on and off above his head. His co-ordination was lousy.

'You'll drop it and set yourself alight, you nutter. Stop it!'

'I'm warming myself up.'

'*I'll* warm you up.' I rubbed his icy arms and blue fingers. He held onto my hands, pulling me down beside him.

'What are you playing at?'

'Keep me company, eh, Tracy?'

'Can't we go in the warm?'

'I like it cold. Kind of numb.'

'Yeah – you're a numskull,' I said, but I lay down properly on the smelly old mattress.

It was so damp it seemed to be seeping 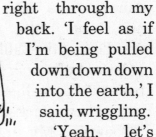 right through my back. 'I feel as if I'm being pulled down down down into the earth,' I said, wriggling.

'Yeah, let's stay down here together, eh? You and me in our own little world.'

I wondered about staying in this garden home for ever. Football and I would lie on our backs on the mattress like marble statues on a tomb and ivy would grow over us and squirrels would scamper past and birds nest in our hair and we wouldn't move a muscle, totally out of it.

But I want to be *in* it. I've got to the fairytale ending of my story. I'm all set to live happily ever after.

'Come on! Getting-up time! Let's play football.' I found the ball and bounced it at Football's head to bring him to his senses.

Football scrambled to his feet, swearing. He tried to grab the ball but I was too quick for him.

'I'm Tracy Beaker the Great and I'm running like the wind, and wow, look, *I've* got the ball!'

'Get out of it, *I'm* the greatest,' Football said. He tried to tackle me. His great boot kicked me instead of the ball.

'Ooowww! My ankle! You're the greatest biggest booted bully!'

'I'm sorry.' Football peered at my leg. 'Red,' he said, sounding puzzled.

'It's blood!'

'I didn't mean to,' Football mumbled.

'Oh yes,' I said, busy dabbing and mopping. 'Like you had no control whatsoever over your foot, it just developed this wicked will of its own and gouged a huge lump out of my flesh. It *hurts*!'

'I'm really really sorry, Tracy.' Football looked like he was nearly in tears. 'I'd never try to hurt you. You mean a lot to me, kid. Tracy?' He tried to put his arm round me.

I dodged underneath. 'Get off me!'

'Go on, you know you like me too.'

'Not when you're all damp and smelly. Yuck, you don't half need a bath, Football.'

'Don't nag at me. You sound like my mum. You're all the same. Nag moan whine whinge. Think I really care about you? You're mad. I don't want you one little bit. No-one wants you, Tracy Beaker.'

'My *mum* wants me!' I yelled.

I roared it so loudly the birds flew into the air in terror and people stopped dead in their tracks all over town and cars ran into each other and aeroplanes stalled in the sky.

'MY MUM WANTS ME!'

Mum's Home (Again)

Mum's home was a little bit different this time. Mum was a little bit different too. She was very pale underneath her make-up and she wore dark glasses and when we had our big hug hello she smelt stale underneath her lovely powdery scent. Her home smelt too, of cigarettes and a lot of booze. The curtains were still drawn.

I went to open them but Mum stopped me. 'Not too much daylight, sweetie,' she said, holding her forehead.

'Have you got a hangover, Mum?'

'What? No, of course not. Don't be silly, darling. No, I have this nasty migraine. I get them a lot. I'm bothered with my nerves.' She lit a cigarette and drew on it desperately.

'I don't make you nervous, do I, Mum?' I asked.

'Don't be so silly, sweetie,' said Mum. 'Now, see what your mum's got for you.'

'Another present!'

I hoped it wasn't chocolates again because I was feeling a bit sick. I was bothered with my nerves too. I take after my mum.

The present was a big parcel, but soft and floppy. *Not* chocolates.

'Is it a rag doll or a teddy?' I asked cautiously, feeling for heads or paws under the wrapping paper.

'Have a look.'

So I carefully undid the wrapping paper, Ultra-neatly this time, and discovered an amazing pair of combat trousers – with a label to die for!

'Oh wow! Great!' I said, whirling around, clutching the trousers, making each leg dance up and down.

'You like them?' said Mum.

'I *love* them. They're seriously cool. Shame I haven't got a really great jacket to go with them.'

'You're not hinting, by any chance?' said Mum, smiling.

I decided to hint for all I was worth. 'Of

course, my old trainers are going to spoil the whole sharp look,' I said. 'I need a pair of Nikes to kind of complete the outfit.'

'I'm not made of money,' said Mum. 'I think it's a bit rich – ha, a bit *poor* – that Cam gets paid a fortune to look after you, while I won't get a penny.'

'Still, I'm worth it, aren't I, Mum?' I said, whirling closer.

'Of course you are, sweetheart,' she said. 'Do give over thumping about though, you're doing my head in.'

I made her a strong black coffee and she sat on her sofa and sipped. Then she lay back on the cushion and stayed very still, not answering when I spoke to her. It looked like she'd fallen asleep, though I couldn't see her eyes for the dark glasses.

I circled the sofa slowly, looking at her, still not quite able to believe she was really my mum and we were with each other and we were going to be together for ever and ever. I'd made it up so many times that it was hard to believe it was real now. I kept staring and staring until my eyes went blurry but Mum didn't vanish: she stretched out in her sparkly sweater and leopardskin pants, so splendid, so special, so sweet to me. So sleepy too.

She wouldn't wake up. I loved to look at her but it started to get just a weeny bit boring. I went for a wander round the room, emptying the ashtrays into the wastebin and taking the glass and empty bottle out into the kitchen like a real Mummy's Little Helper. I had a peer in all her kitchen cupboards and the fridge but there weren't many snacks to nibble on, just frozen packets and diet stuff and booze.

I played hopscotch across the kitchen tiles for a bit and then I took off my trainers and played ice skating and then I shuffled back to the living room hopefully because I heard Mum sigh, but she'd just turned over and was still playing Sleeping Beauty. One of her black suede high heels had fallen off. I tried it on, and then carefully eased the other one off her foot too. I had my very own pair of high heels. I clonked about the living room for a bit to get my balance and then staggered off to her bedroom to admire myself in her wardrobe mirror.

I had a little peep in her wardrobe – and

before I could stop myself I was
dressing up in her mohair sweater and
her leather skirt. I looked almost like
my mum! I pretended to be her. I
promised my little Tracy I would always
love her and be with her for ever no
matter what.

Then *my* mum came into the bedroom,
rubbing her eyes and lighting her fag. 'So
that's where you've got to. Did I doze off for
five minutes? Hey, you cheeky baggage,
you're all togged up in my clothes! Take them
off! And watch that skirt, it cost a fortune.'

'Oh Mum, please, let me keep them on, just
for a second. I look so beautiful. Just like you,'
I begged. I rootled through her wardrobe. 'Oh
wow! I love your red dress. Can I try that on
too? And the purply thing? And what's
this black dress? Oh, it's dead sexy.'

'Tracy!' said Mum, giggling. 'OK
then. Come here, we'll play dressing up.'

It was MAGIC. Mum got me all
beautifully dressed up – though we
both fell about laughing when I tried
the black dress on because it came right
down to my belly button and I wasn't
just topless, I was very nearly bottomless too.

I ended up back in the mohair sweater and the leather skirt and Mum's suede high heels, and she made me up like a real grown-up lady and did my hair too. I strutted about like a fashion model and Mum joined in too, showing me how to do the walk properly, and I did my best to copy her. Then we played being rock stars and Mum was incredible – she could do all the bouncy bits and the little dances and everything, and she could really sing too. She has this amazing voice. She said she was queen of the karaoke night down the pub and everyone always begged her to sing.

'It's karaoke night tonight, actually,' she said.

'Oh great! Can we go? I'd love to see you being the star singer.'

'You can't go to the pub, Tracy, you're just a little kid.'

'I went with Cam and Jane and Liz once. We sat in the garden and I had a cocktail called a St Clement's and three packets of salt and vinegar crisps.'

'Yes, well, my pub hasn't got a garden and you can't sit out in the evening anyway. No, I was wondering about *me* going.'

'But . . . what about me?'

'Well, you can go to bed. I'll make you up a bed on the sofa and then you can watch telly for a bit as a treat.'

'You're going to leave me on my own?' I said, my heart thumping.

'Oh come on, Tracy, you're not a baby,' said Mum.

'I don't really like being left on my own,' I said. 'Mum, can't you stay and play with me?'

'For goodness' sake, Tracy. I've been playing daft games with you for hours! You can't begrudge me an hour or two with my friends down the pub. A couple of drinks, that's all. I'll be home long before closing time, I swear. Anyway, you'll be asleep by then.'

'What if I can't get to sleep?'

'Then watch the telly, like I said.'

'I don't think there's anything good on tonight.'

'Well, watch a video! Honestly – kids! You can tell you've been spoilt. You're going to have to learn to do as you're told if we're going to get along.'

'You're not supposed to leave me.'

'I'll do what I like, young lady. Don't take that tone with me! Do you want me to send you back to the Children's Home?'

I shook my head. I couldn't speak.

'Well then. Don't you get stroppy with me. Out of my clothes and into your jim-jams, right?'

She started treating me like I was a sulky little toddler. She even washed all the make-up off my face herself and then she played silly games with the flannel, pretending it was a bird pecking off my nose. I laughed a lot and went along with the whole charade because I hoped if I was really really good and sweet and cute she'd change her mind and stay home.

But she didn't.

She left me.

She gave me a kiss and tucked me up on the sofa and waved her fingers at me and then she put on her coat and walked off in her black suede high heels.

I called after her. I said she didn't have to play with me, I'd lie watching telly as quiet as

190

a mouse, I'd do anything she wanted, just so long as she stayed with me.

I don't know whether she heard or not. She still went anyway. So I was left. All on my own.

I got angry at first. She wasn't supposed to leave me. If I phoned Elaine and told tales Mum would be in serious trouble. But I didn't want to phone Elaine. I knew who I wanted to phone – but I couldn't. I couldn't let on to Cam that it had all gone wrong so quickly.

Then I got angry with myself. Had it really gone wrong? I didn't know why I was getting in such a state. So what if my mum had slipped out for a drink or two? Lots and lots and lots of mums went down the pub, for goodness' sake. And my mum had been wonderful to me. She'd bought me fantastic new trousers and she'd played games with me for ages. She was the best mum in the world and so why couldn't I just lie back on her lovely comfy sofa and watch telly and have a good time till she came back?

I knew why. I was scared. It reminded me of all those other times when I was little and she left me then. I couldn't remember them properly. I just remembered crying in the dark and no-one coming. The dark seemed to stretch out for ever into space and I was all by myself and Mum was never ever coming back for me.

I felt that way now, even though I knew it was stupid. I scrunched up in a tiny ball on the sofa and I thought about Cam and I wanted her so badly. No, I wanted my mum so badly. I was all muddled. I just felt so lonely, and after a long while I slept but when I woke up Mum still wasn't back even though the pubs had been shut for ages. I switched on the telly but it jabbered away too loudly in the silent flat so I shut it off quick and lay on the sofa, listening and listening, wondering what I would do if Mum never came back. And then when I'd very nearly given up altogether I heard footsteps and giggling and the key turning in the front door.

The light went on in the living room. I kept hunched down, my eyes squeezed shut.

'Whoops! I'd forgotten I'd tucked her up on the sofa!' Mum hissed. 'Funny little thing. Doesn't look a bit like me, does she? Oh dear. Come on, out we go. You'd better go home, sweetie. Yes, I know, but it can't be helped.'

There was a horrible male mumbling, a slurping sound, and more giggles from Mum.

'You naughty thing! No! Shh now, we'll wake the kid.'

I breathed as slowly and evenly as I could. The man was mumbling again.

'Oooh!' said Mum. 'Yes, I'd love to go to the races on Saturday. Great idea! Though . . . well, my little Tracy will still be here. She can come too, can't she? She won't be any trouble, I swear.'

Mumble mumble, fumble fumble.

'I know it wouldn't be so much fun. What? I *see*. So we'd be staying the whole weekend? It does sound tempting. Go on, then, you've twisted my arm. I'll fix it.'

My eyes were still tight shut but I couldn't stop them leaking. It was OK. They didn't see. They weren't looking at me.

I was awake long before Mum in the morning. I had my bag all packed, ready. I wondered how she was going to break it to me, whether she'd tell me it straight or spin me some story.

It was the story. With a lot of spin on it. She came out with it at breakfast. I was amazed. It was the sort of stuff I made up when I was about six, the most pathetic never-ever tale about bumping into a film producer down the pub and how he was bowled over by her and he was giving her this big acting chance and he needed her to meet up with all his big-film-guy cronies at the weekend, *this* weekend, and she knew this weekend was the most special ever because we were supposed to be together but on the other hand we could spend every other weekend of our lives together but this weekend was her one chance of finding fame and fortune and I did understand, didn't I, sweetie?

I understood. I looked at my mum – really really looked at her – and I understood everything. I didn't have it out with her. I just made my lips turn up and said that of course I understood and I wished her luck. She went a bit  watery-eyed then, so that her last-night's mascara smudged, and she reached across the table so that her black nylon nightie dripped in my cornflakes and she gave me a big hug. I breathed in her warm powdery smell one last time. Then she gave me a little pat, ran her fingers through her rumpled hair, plucked at her soggy nightie, and said she'd better go and have a bath and get herself all prettied up and what did I want to do today, darling?

I knew what I was going to do. As soon as Mum was in the bath I went to her handbag, nicked some money, picked up my bag and scarpered.

I left her a note.

The note got a bit smeared and blotchy but there wasn't time to write it out again. I needed to leave her a message so she'd know I wasn't a thief.

> It's OK, Mum. I know you don't really want me. I'll be fine. I've taken ten pounds for travelling but I'll save up and send it you back, honest. Thanks for everything.
>
> With lots of love
> from Tracy
> xxx

Then I walked out, closing her front door ever so slowly so she wouldn't hear. Then I ran. And ran and ran and ran.

I didn't know where I was going. I didn't really have any place to go.

I could go back to Cam but she probably wouldn't want me back now. Not after all the things I said. I came out with all sorts of stuff. Things that I didn't want to write in this book. Things to hurt her. It was so hard choosing between Cam and my mum so I made it easy by doing such dreadful things to Cam that she'd never ever want me back.

Only I made the wrong choice. Now I haven't got anywhere to go.

Yes I have.

I know where I'm going.

The Smashed Home

I found my way, easy-peasy. I got a train and then a bus and I had lunch in McDonald's. It was great.

I don't need ANYONE to look after me. I don't need my mum. I don't need Cam. I can look after myself, no bother at all. And it isn't as if I haven't got a roof over my head. I've got a whole house. All to myself.

Well. Sometimes I share it. Someone had been doing some serious housekeeping. There were cans of Coke and Kit-kats in the 'fridge' in the kitchen, and a cardboard dustpan and brush that really worked – sort of. But the living room was the real picture. A brand new television, with a video recorder too. A table with a permanent embroidered tablecloth and place settings. Three chairs, all different sizes, like the Three Bears story – a big one for

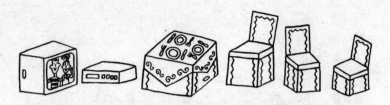

Football, a medium size for me and the littlest for Alexander. Alexander himself, sitting on a special rug, was making yet more Ideal Home delights.

'Tracy!' he said, his eyes lighting up.

It felt so good that someone was pleased to see me that I gave his bony little shoulder a squeeze. 'Hi, Chippendale,' I said.

Alexander peered at me. 'Chip . . . ?' he said. 'Aren't they those big oily men who take off all their clothes? Are you teasing me?'

'Hey, Alexander, you're the one who's supposed to be the brainbox. I mean Chippendale as in *furniture*. He was some old guy in history who made posh chairs, right?'

'Oh, I *see*,' said Alexander, busily slotting one piece of cardboard into two grooves.

'Another chair, maestro?'

'No, I'm making a bookcase this time. I thought it would be great to have a bookcase. So we could keep our books in it. I could keep my *Alexander the Great* book here. And you could keep your diary in it.'

'*What* diary?'

'Well, whatever you write in your big fat purple book.'

'If you've been peeking in my big fat purple book I'll poke your eyes out!'

'I wouldn't dare, Tracy. Oops!' Alexander rolled his eyes. 'No more dares, eh?'

'Not for the moment, anyway. So. What are you doing here, Alexander? I thought you weren't going to come any more.'

'I know. My dad will kill me when he finds out I've been bunking off again. But when I went back to school I limped for all I was worth but Mr Cochran, he's the games master, he said I was a pathetic little weed and I had to play anyway. So I tried. And I got pushed over. And it hurt a lot so my eyes watered. And then everyone said I was crying and that just proved how weedy and wet I am and someone said "Gherkin is a jerkin" and they all started chanting it and—'

'I get the general picture,' I said. 'Still. It's not like it's the end of the world.'

'It kind of feels that way to me.'

'Some silly stuck-up kids call you names. And one of the teachers picks on you. Oh boo hoo! That's *nothing*. You want to hear what some of the kids at my school call me. And Miss Vomit Bagley has *really* got it in for me. She picks on me all the time – when I'm there. I bet some of your teachers think you're the bee's knees because you're a right old swotty brainbox.'

'Well . . .' Alexander considered. 'Yes, Mr Bernstein and Mr Rogers like me, and Mrs Betterstall says I'm—'

'Yeah yeah yeah. See? And I bet your horrible old dad really cares about you or he wouldn't go on so. I haven't even *got* a dad, have I?'

'You've got a mum though,' said Alexander, slotting the last cardboard shelf into place. He stood the bookcase up for me to admire – and then saw my face. He suddenly remembered. 'Oh! Your mum!'

'What about her?' I said fiercely.

'You were meant to be staying with her.'

'Yeah. Well. I got a bit fed up, if you must know.'

'Didn't she buy you all that stuff you wanted?'

'Yes, she did. She bought me heaps and heaps. Look!' I did a twirl in my new combat trousers.

'Oh yes,' said Alexander quickly. 'The trousers. Yes. They look super-cool. You look lovely, Tracy.'

'No I don't,' I said, sitting down beside him. 'I look funny. My mum says.'

'Well, you *are* funny,' said Alexander. 'That's good, isn't it? Tracy . . . what went wrong with you and your mum?' He patted my knee timidly. 'Didn't she like you?'

I jerked away from him. 'Nothing went wrong. I told you. My mum's crazy about me. She can't make enough of a fuss of me. But after a bit I just thought, hey, who needs this? I don't need *her*.'

'Ah! You need *Cam*, don't you?' said Alexander, looking immensely pleased. 'I'm right, aren't I?'

'No!' I folded my arms. 'You're wrong wrong wrong. I don't need her.'

Alexander still wouldn't be squashed. 'Well, you need me. And Football. We're your friends.'

'I don't need you either. I don't need no-one.'

201

'That's a double negative. If you don't need *no*-one it means you need *some*one, don't you see?'

'I see that you're the most annoying little Smartypants and it's no wonder everyone picks on you. You really get on my nerves.' I gave him a push. Then I gave his bookcase a push too.

'Watch my bookcase!' said Alexander.

'It's a rubbish bookcase,' I said, and my fist went thump thump thump.

'My bookcase!' Alexander wailed.

'It's *my* house and I don't want your stupid bookcase in it, see?'

'I'll make one specially for you,' Alexander offered, trying to slot his shelves back into place.

'I don't want you to make anything for me. I don't need *anything*. It's my house and I don't want a single rubbish thing in it. I'm sick of homes, I'm sick of stuff. I want it to be *empty*.' I smashed his stupid bookcase flat and then I whirled round the living room, breaking up all Alexander's furniture.

'Don't, Tracy! Don't! Don't!' Alexander shouted.

I smashed. Alexander screamed. Football

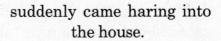

suddenly came haring into the house.

'What is it? What's going on? You two all right?' he said. He looked about him. 'Who's turned the place over?'

'Oh Football, thank goodness!' said Alexander, clinging to him. 'Stop Tracy. She's wrecking everything. Even my new bookcase.'

'Sounds a good idea to me,' said Football, shaking Alexander off. 'Yeah, let's have a bit of fun, right, Tracy? What you doing here anyway? Didn't your mum want you after all?'

'You shut up, Football.' I glared at him. 'Your mum doesn't want you. And neither does your precious dad.'

I had to hurt everyone to show I didn't need any of them. So they couldn't hurt me. 'How's your dad, Football? How's your dad, Alexander?' I said.

'Quit it,' said Football.

'Why don't we *all* quit it?' Alexander begged. 'Let's make friends and . . . and mend the furniture.'

'Shut up, Gherkin,' said Football. 'Who cares about your boring old furniture?' He flicked his dad's lighter, waving it at the crumpled bookcase.

'Stop it!' Alexander shouted.

'Don't tell *me* to stop anything!' said Football, flicking again.

The flame leapt at the cardboard, singeing it for a second and then suddenly flaming.

'You're *crazy*!' said Alexander.

'Shut up,' said Football, stamping just in time.

'You'll set yourself alight! You'll set the whole place on fire,' Alexander cried. 'You mustn't ever ever ever play with fire.'

'Oooh, aren't I *naughty*!' said Football, imitating Alexander's high-pitched voice.

I giggled and Football grinned at me.

'Let's liven this dump up, eh, Tracy?' he said. He threw the lighter to me. 'Your turn.'

'Don't, Tracy. Don't be so *stupid*,' Alexander begged.

'I dare you, Tracy,' said Football.

I swallowed, the lighter hot in my hand.

'You mustn't, Tracy. You can't start that

awful Dare Game again. *Please* don't dare. You know it's crazy!'

Of course I knew it was crazy. But I *felt* crazy.

I suddenly flicked the lighter and held it to my small cardboard-box chair. A sudden flame leapt in the air. I went to stamp it out – but I wasn't big enough.

'Don't! You'll burn yourself!' Alexander screamed.

Football tried to elbow me out the way but I was determined to win this dare. I seized the flattened bookcase and beat hard at the flame – and it went out.

'There! I did it! I won the dare!' I yelled, leaping around and punching the air.

'That's great, kid. You and me, we're the greatest,' yelled Football.

'You're the greatest *idiots*,' said Alexander tearfully.

'You always try to spoil everything, Alexander,' I said. 'Go on. It's your turn now. I dare you.'

'No!'

'Come on, you've got to, if I dare you.' I

tried to pass him the lighter but he put his fists behind his back.

'I'm not going to. It's mad and dangerous,' said Alexander.

'He hasn't got the bottle,' said Football, sneering.

'Go on, Alexander,' I said. 'You felt great last time after you jumped out the window.'

Alexander shook his head violently. 'I was mad then. What if the mattress hadn't been there? I'd have been killed. I'm not taking any more chances.'

'Coward! Chicken!'

'Cluck cluck cluck!'

'You can cluck and call me all the names you like,' said Alexander. 'I'm still not going to do it.'

'Because you're too scared,' I said.

'You're only doing it because *you're* scared,' said Alexander. 'Scared Football won't think you as tough as he is. Only he's scared too.'

'*I'm* scared?' said Football, outraged. 'Who am I scared of, Gherkin?' He took the lighter from me and stood in front of Alexander, flicking it on and off, on and off. 'Am I scared of you, is that it? Or scared of skinny little

Tracy? I'm not scared of anyone, you stupid jerk.'

Alexander still didn't give up. 'You're scared your dad doesn't care about you any more, that's what you're scared of.'

I couldn't help nodding. 'Ah! He's got you there, Football.'

'No he hasn't. I'm not scared. I don't give a toss about my dad any more,' said Football.

'Yes you do,' said Alexander relentlessly. 'That's why you act crazy – because it's *driving* you crazy.'

'You think you know it all but you don't know anything,' Football shouted. 'Now button that lippy little mouth of yours or I'll set light to *you*.'

'You wouldn't dare!' Alexander squealed.

'Shut *up*, Alexander,' I said.

'I'll dare anything,' Football declared, waving his lighter round wildly.

Alexander snatched a cardboard shelf and held it up like a shield. Football lunged forward, expecting Alexander to dodge backwards. Alexander stood still – and there was a sudden flare of flame. Alexander stared, open-mouthed, unable to move.

I snatched the sizzling cardboard, threw it to the floor, and stamped on it.

'*Stop* it, Football!' I shouted. 'This is getting too scary now.'

'You can't stop me. No-one can stop me,' said Football. 'I'll show you, Tracy Beaker. I'll show you, Gherkin.'

'Why do you have to bully us? We're your *friends*,' Alexander said desperately.

'I don't need no friends,' said Football.

'No, Football, you can't say "no" friends because it's a double neg— aaaaah!' Alexander was cut off in mid-grammatical quibble because Football grabbed him by the front of his shirt with one hand. His *other* hand was still waving in the air, clutching the lighter. Alexander suddenly made a grab for it – snatched it – and then threw it wildly. It sailed right across the room and out the window.

'My lighter! My dad's lighter!' Football yelled, letting go of Alexander in his shock.

'Oh help! I didn't mean it to go out the window. I didn't know I could throw that far!' said Alexander.

'I'll kill you, Gherkin!' said Football, his eyes popping, his face purple.

'Run!' I yelled to Alexander. 'Get out the house, quick!'

Alexander ran – but he wasn't quick enough. Football caught him before he was even out the door. He raised his big fist ready to give him a punch – but I got there first. I shoved Alexander as hard as I could out the way and grabbed Football from behind.

'Don't you dare, you big bully!' I yelled.

Alexander collapsed in a heap and started whimpering. Football and I took no notice, too busy fighting.

'Get *off*, Tracy! Ouch! Don't you dare kick me!'

'I'll dare anything, same as you! You think you're so big and tough but I'll show you!' I kicked him again, wishing my trainers were socking great Doc Martens.

'You little whatsit!' said Football, nearly knocking me over.

I hit out hard, catching him right where it hurts most.

'Oooooomph!' said Football, doubling up. 'No wonder your mum doesn't want you. No-one could ever want you, Tracy Beaker.'

'No-one wants you either! Especially not your precious dad. He doesn't give a toss about you. It's obvious.'

'You shut up!' He wrestled me to the floor.

'*You* shut up, you stupid snot-nosed bully,' I gasped, kicking out from under him. 'That's all you can do, isn't it? Hit out at people. You think you're so great but you're useless. You're even useless at football.'

'Shut up or I'll bang your head on the floor!'

'You try!'

Football tried. It hurt like hell. So I spat hard. Upwards, right in his face.

Football stared down at me, wondrously spattered. 'You wouldn't dare do that again!'

I did.

'You dirty little monkey!' he said, banging my head again.

'It'll be right in your eye next!' I warned.

'I'll spit right back, *I'm* warning *you*!'

'Go on, then. I dare you!'

He dared all right. It was totally disgusting. I went to spit back but my mouth was too dry. 'I've run out of spit! It's not fair. Wait!' I tried but only managed the merest dribble.

'That was a bit pathetic!' said Football.

'You just wait. Oooh! I keep blowing raspberries instead of spitting.'

'Can't even spit!' Football jeered.

'Just give me a few seconds.'

'So I'm going to hang around waiting?' said Football, leaning back.

'Come *here*, Football!' I commanded, trying to summon up more spit by smacking my lips and sucking in my cheeks.

'You look like you're about to give me a great big kiss with your lips like that!' Football grinned.

'Yuck!' I couldn't help giggling at the very idea.

'You watch out or I'll kiss you!' said Football.

'No you don't!' I said, trying to wriggle free. 'Hey, come on, get off me, you big lump.'

Football did as he was told this time. The fight was over.

'I didn't hurt you, did I?' Football asked, picking me up and brushing me down.

'Oh *no*, whacking great kicks on the shin and bashes on the bonce don't hurt a *bit!*'

'You twit,' said Football. 'Hey, we made a poem!' He looked at Alexander. 'And you're a nit! There. You're in the poem too. Hey, Gherkin, we've stopped fighting. You can get up now.'

'It's OK, Alexander. Alexander? Are you all right?'

'N-o-o-o!' said Alexander, still lying on the floor, his leg stuck out at an odd angle.

 'I didn't hurt *you*, did I?' said Football, looking stricken.

'It was – when – Tracy – knocked me – over. My *leg!*' Alexander gasped.

'Oh help!' I said. 'Stand up, Alexander, and let me have a look.'

'I can't. I really can't.'

I bent over him. I saw his leg. 'Oh no, Alexander! I've really hurt your leg! It's all bendy. How terrible! What am I going to do?'

'I think – better – get me – to hospital,' Alexander mumbled.

I tried to help him up. Alexander groaned with the pain.

'Here, I'll carry you. Come here, little guy. Don't worry, I'll be ever so gentle,' said Football, putting Alexander over his shoulder in a fireman's lift.

'Oh Alexander,' I said, holding his hand. '*Please* be all right. I can't stand it if I've hurt you. You're my best friend in all the world. Please please please get better!'

Alexander's Real Home

We took Alexander to hospital. Football was willing to carry him the whole way but I still had some money from Mum's wallet so we took a taxi.

The taxi driver sighed when he saw Alexander. 'You kids been rough-housing?' he said, shaking his head.

Alexander looked delighted to be thought capable of roughing up a house. He was very brave. He was obviously in terrible pain, his face greeny-white, his fringe sticking to his sweaty forehead, but he didn't cry at all.

We waited with him at the hospital until he was whisked away in a wheelchair to the X-ray department.

'We'd better get going then,' said Football. 'They've phoned for his parents. I don't fancy meeting up with them. Especially the dad.'

'But we've got to wait to see if Alexander's all right!'

'Of course he'll be all right. He's in hospital,' said Football. He looked round the bleak orange waiting room and shuddered. 'I hate hospitals. They give me the creeps. I'm off.' He stood up. 'Come on, Tracy.'

'No. I'm waiting.'

'He'll be all right. It's just a broken leg. The nurse said.'

'How would you feel if you'd "just" broken your leg, Football?' I asked.

'Well. It would be tragic for me, seeing as it would affect my game. But Alexander's hardly going to bother, is he?' Football sat down again, sighing. 'I hate hospitals.'

'So you keep saying.'

'The way they look. All them long corridors and lots of doors with scary things going on behind them.'

'So close your eyes.'

'I can still smell I'm in hospital.' He sniffed and pulled a terrible face. 'It's making me feel sick.'

'How do you think Alexander feels *behind* one of the scary doors?' I said severely.

Football hunched down lower on his plastic chair. 'He's a weird little chap,' he said. 'He breaks his leg – well, you break it for him – and he hardly makes a sound. I've seen really tough nuts in agony on the football pitch, effing and blinding, even sobbing. Not old Alexander. He's really . . . brave?'

'I didn't *mean* to break his leg!'

'Yeah, I know, but I still think it's mad to hang around here. His mum and dad aren't going to be too pleased with you.'

'It was just one little push. I wasn't trying to hurt him, I was simply trying to get him out the way. I can't bear it that it's all my fault.' I started crying, snivelling and snorting like a baby – even though I never ever cry.

Football looked all round, embarrassed. 'Don't, Tracy, people are staring,' he hissed, giving me a nudge.

I went on crying noisily.

'Here, haven't you got a hankie?'

I shook my head, past caring that I had tears dripping down my face and a very runny nose.

Football darted across the room. I thought it had got too much and he was running away – but he dashed into the toilet and came back with a wad of loo-roll.

'Here,' he said, dabbing at my face. 'Don't cry so, Tracy. It wasn't really your fault at all. It was mine. I was the one who really lost it back at the house. I was out my mind setting all that stuff on fire.' He paused. 'Do you think I'm really crazy, Tracy?'

'Yes!' I said, blowing my nose. Then I relented. 'No, not really. Just a little bit bonkers.'

'Do you think I should get some kind of treatment?'

'You're fine, Football. It's Alexander we've got to worry about right now. I just don't get it. One little push, he falls over and breaks his leg. Yet when he falls off the roof he doesn't so much as break his big toe. He bobs up again as right as rain. He's a marvel, little Alexander.' I gave my face another mop. 'He *is* going to be all right, isn't he, Football?'

'Of course he is. It's only a broken leg.'

'Yes, but it might have been *badly* broken. It looked all funny and sticky-out in the wrong place. What if they can't set it properly? What if *infection* sets in? And his leg goes all mouldy and maggoty and has to be cut off?'

'Shut *up*, Tracy. That couldn't happen. Could it?'

'We didn't even notice. We were too busy fighting,' I wailed.

'You're a fierce little fighter, Tracy,' said Football.

'I'm going to give up fighting now. I hate it that Alexander got hurt.'

I sighed, wondering exactly what they were doing to Alexander. Football sighed too. We took it in turns. I fidgeted. Football fidgeted.

I stood up to stretch my legs – and nearly bumped into a couple who came rushing into the waiting room. The man was very big and bossy-looking with a briefcase. The lady was small and timid with a little twitchy mouse face. I didn't need three guesses to work out who they were. I whizzed back to my seat sharpish.

'I believe our son Alexander has been brought into Casualty,' the man said to a nurse.

'Please can we see him? Is he really all right?' the woman said, nearly in tears.

They were led along the corridor. Football let out a huge sigh. So did I.

'Time to get going, Tracy,' said Football.

I knew it was the wisest option. But I *had* to wait to see if Alexander was all right, even if it meant being beaten up by Briefcase Guy for injuring his son. Maybe I almost wanted to get into serious trouble with Alexander's parents. I felt I deserved it.

Football thought this was crazy – but he stayed too.

We waited and we waited and we waited. And waited some more. And then suddenly we heard Alexander's little piping voice

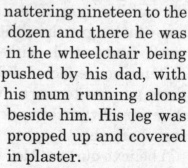 nattering nineteen to the dozen and there he was in the wheelchair being pushed by his dad, with his mum running along beside him. His leg was propped up and covered in plaster.

'Alexander! How *are* you?' I said, charging up to him.

'Tracy! And Football! You waited for me all this time!' Alexander said excitedly. 'Mum, Dad, these are my friends.'

'Alexander's been telling us all about you,' said his mum.

'Yes, we should really give all of you a severe telling-off,' said his dad ominously.

'I *told* you we should have scarpered,' Football muttered.

'It was my fault,' I said. I meant to sound bold and brave but my voice went all high and squeaky so they didn't hear me properly.

'It's very silly to play truant. I'm sure you'll be in as much trouble with your schools as Alexander is with his,' said his dad, wagging his finger at Football and me. 'But I suppose I'm pleased you've all made friends. Alexander's always found it so hard to make friends because he's so shy.'

'You've been such good friends too,' said his mum. 'Alexander's told us all about his accident – how you were so kind and sensible when he tripped over. Other children might have run away and left him but you picked him up and looked after him and got him to the hospital. We're so grateful to you.'

Football and I shifted from one foot to the

other. We looked at Alexander. He grinned back at us.

'Alexander's our best ever friend,' I said.

'Yeah. He's our mate,' said Football. 'So – you're OK now, right?'

'Does he *look* all right?' I said, elbowing Football impatiently.

Football shrugged. 'I suppose that sounded a bit dumb,' he admitted. 'Seeing as he's in plaster almost up to his bum. Hey, poetry again!'

'You didn't sound at *all* dumb, Football,' said Alexander. 'Well, you couldn't literally *sound* dumb, but anyway. I *am* OK now. I've just fractured my tibia.'

'But you've hurt your leg!' said Football.

'Ultra-dumb!' I said. 'The tibia's a bone in his leg. And you've got a bone in your head, Football.'

'But you won't have to stay in a wheelchair for ever?' said Football.

'Oh no, dear,' said Alexander's mum. 'This is just while we're in the hospital. Alexander should be able to hobble about, using a crutch.'

'But I won't be able to walk properly for six whole weeks until the plaster comes off,' said Alexander.

'Six whole weeks! That's awful,' said Football.

'No, it's not, it's brilliant,' said Alexander, eyes shining. 'I won't be able to play games.'

'Really, Alexander,' said his dad, sighing impatiently.

'I'd die if I couldn't play football for six weeks!' said Football. 'I've been doing my nut stuck here for hours and hours not being able to kick my ball about.'

Alexander's dad nodded approvingly. 'How on earth did you two boys become chums?' he said.

'Do you go to Alexander's school?' his mum asked.

'They don't *go* to school, that's the point,' said Alexander's dad. 'What do your parents say?'

Football stuck out his lip. 'They don't care. Not my mum.' He paused. 'Nor my dad.'

Alexander leaned forward. 'I'm sorry I threw your precious lighter away, Football. Maybe you'll be able to find it in the garden.'

'Maybe. Still. It don't really matter. My dad's thrown *me* away, hasn't he?'

'What about you, Curly?' said Alexander's dad to me. 'Surely your mother and father worry themselves sick about a little girl like you roaming the streets?'

'I haven't got a dad. And . . . and I don't expect I'll see much of my mum now,' I mumbled.

'Tracy's fostered,' Alexander explained.

They all stared at me. It's a wonder they didn't try to pat me on the head. I glared back.

'How about coming home with us for tea?' said Alexander's mum. 'You too, dear,' she added, nodding at Football a little warily.

'Yes, do come,' Alexander begged. 'My mum's mega-good at baking. Can we have chocolate cake, Mum?'

Football seemed keen on the idea. His own tea was usually just a trip down to the chippie. I was equally happy to go along with things seeing as I was starving hungry (it seemed months since I'd munched my Big Mac) and I didn't have any home of my own to go to.

We helped Alexander out onto the hospital steps. His dad went to get the car and his mum returned the wheelchair to the ward. Football and I supported Alexander, one on either side.

'You're a real gem for not telling your mum and dad it was all my fault,' I whispered, and I gave him a quick kiss on the cheek.

'It was my fault really,' said Football. 'I kept picking on you. But I won't any more, I swear.'

I could feel Alexander trembling. His face was peony red. 'You're both *really* my friends? You're not kidding me? This is so great!'

'*You're* great. Alexander the Great. Though you're also crazy, because your so-called friends have broken your leg,' I said.

'Yeah, you've had to spend hours and hours in hospital,' said Football.

'I like it in hospital,' said Alexander. 'It's been ever so interesting. The doctor showed me the X-ray and explained all about bones and it was fascinating. I think I might be a doctor when I grow up. So I suppose I'd really better stop bunking off school or I won't pass my exams. You have to get top grades to do Medicine. And school won't be anywhere near as bad if I'm off games for six whole weeks. Then you'll just have to push me hard again, Tracy, so I can break my other leg.'

'It was only a *little* push!'

'I know. I fell awkwardly. I *am* awkward.

That's why I'm so useless at football. My legs don't work the right way.'

'Your head's fine though,' said Football. 'Here, maybe I'll train you to do my famous Bonce-Buster so you can head the ball into the back of the net, easy-peasy.'

'That would be great,' said Alexander.

'That would be a blooming miracle,' I said.

Alexander and Football seemed to be bonding like Superglue. They chatted together in the car all the way to Alexander's home.

It was a *huge* house, one of those big black and white ones with criss-cross windows and neat little trees in tubs on either side of the front door. We hadn't realized quite how posh Alexander is. Things got even ritzier inside, with polished wood everywhere and matching sofas and chairs so vigorously tidied with cushions at exact angles that I only dared perch on the end of a hard chair with red and white stripes like toothpaste. Football stayed in the middle of the carpet standing on the outside edge of his trainers, his ball clasped close to his chest.

Alexander's mum got Alexander tucked up on an armchair with his bad leg propped on a footstool, and then she went away to make us all tea.

Alexander's dad gave us another one of his lectures about bunking off school and it all got seriously *heavy* and Alexander's face was as white and stiff as his plaster and Football rested his chin on his ball and I slid down the red and white stripes till my bottom was off the seat altogether. But then Alexander's mum came darting back with juice and home-made chocolate chip cookies which livened things up a little. I thought this was tea but it turned out this was just to keep us going until she'd cooked the *real* tea. She wanted Football and me to ring home to explain we were out for tea so no-one would worry. Football said his mum was at work so she wouldn't know – and added under his breath that she couldn't care less anyway.

'And what about your foster mother, Tracy, dear?' said Alexander's mum.

'She won't worry either, honestly,' I said firmly, though Alexander frowned at me.

Football had to drop his football to cope with his juice and cookie. His ball started rolling away so he gave it a nifty little kick up onto his trainer and back again.

'That was neat footwork, lad,' said Alexander's dad.

'Football's brilliant at football, Dad,' said Alexander proudly.

'I'm not bad,' Football mumbled, surprisingly bashful.

Alexander's dad started talking soccer-speak and after a few sentences Football joined in, and even demonstrated a few of his party tricks.

'Ooh dear, you will watch the ornaments, won't you?' said Alexander's mum, rushing back with bowls of crisps and saucers of Smarties.

'How about if we nip out into the garden, lad?' said Alexander's dad.

They went out through the French windows and almost immediately they were kicking the ball backwards and forwards like old pals.

Alexander peered at them a little wistfully. 'My dad likes Football,' he said.

'He likes you too, Alexander. Underneath.'

Alexander frowned and shook his head.

'Well, your mum definitely likes you.'

Alexander gave a little nod.

'And Football likes you. And *I* like you lots and lots. You do know that, don't you, Alexander?'

He seemed to. His head was bobbing about like he was little Noddy. 'I like you too, Tracy,' he said. 'And Football likes you ever so. He wants you to be his girlfriend.'

'Well. I'm not so sure about that,' I said. 'I *might* be his girlfriend. But I'll be your girlfriend too. If you want.'

'I do want! And – and your mum maybe can't always like you, but Cam does. It sounds like she really really cares about you.'

'No she doesn't. Anyway. I've blown it with her.'

I let myself think properly about Cam. All the stuff we did together. Daft things – like we'd dance to *Top of the Pops* and we'd shout out silly answers to the quizzes and we'd invent all sorts of new rude funny things to happen in all the soaps. And at night Cam would always tuck me up and ruffle my hair. And if I got scared at night – a bad dream or something – I could always go and climb into her bed. She'd moan and go, 'Oh Tracy Fidget

Bottom,' but she'd still cuddle me close. And though her food was so boring and healthy she took me to McDonald's too. And when I didn't get invited to Roxanne's party at school Cam said we could have our own private party just us two instead and we even had birthday cake.

It wasn't all Party Time of course. She could get dead narked sometimes and do a real moody on me – but then I suppose I could get a bit stroppy at times too. She didn't ever leave me alone at home. She didn't go off with any men. And one time when she was going to this very special concert with Jane and Liz and another friend was looking after me, Cam cancelled because I had this stomach upset. Imagine, she gave up going to a concert to mop up all my sick.

We got on OK, Cam and me. Like real friends. Sisters. Almost . . . almost like she was my mum.

It was weird. Alexander's mum fixed us this most magnificent tea ever, with pizza

triangles and quiche
fingers and little
sausages and amazing
chocolate cake and a
sponge with pink icing
too and ice cream with

special strawberry sauce – but when it was in
my mouth it all tasted like Alexander's cardboard.

I couldn't chew properly because I had this
big lump in my throat.

I wanted to go *home*.

Home Sweet Home

So I did go home. Alexander's dad insisted on driving me back to Cam's. He took Football too and they were still so busy nattering about football that they didn't notice I was getting quieter and quieter until I said nothing at all for the last five minutes.

I jumped out the car and waved goodbye to them and then I stared at the door and put my finger on the bell like I was actually pressing it. I heard the car drive off behind me. I stayed standing still with my finger hovering above the bell until my entire arm went numb. I rehearsed again and again in my head the things I was going to say. They all sounded stupid. I decided I couldn't say anything. I couldn't face seeing Cam because I was sure she'd push me away and tell me to clear off.

I would if she'd treated me the way I'd treated her.

I couldn't go back to my own mum. But I didn't have to wander the streets or crouch on cardboard furniture in our empty house. I knew the social services emergency number. I could summon Elaine within the hour and she'd be able to find me a bed for the night and get cracking on my case in the morning. Social workers don't ever give up on you. She'd grit her bunny teeth and do her level best to find me a new home.

But I didn't want a new home. I knew what I wanted even though it was too late. My finger suddenly stabbed all by itself and the bell rang and rang and rang. Then I heard footsteps running and the door flew open and there was Cam, her hair sticking up and her eyes red and her cardie on all the wrong buttons and yet she suddenly looked the most wonderful woman in the whole world.

'Cam!'

'Tracy!'

I leapt up at her and threw my arms round her neck and she hugged me tighter than tight and we held each other as if we could never ever bear to let go. I was dimly aware that Jane and Liz came out into the hall and joined in the hug for a moment and then they patted Cam on the back and ruffled my hair and then let themselves out the door, leaving Cam and me on our own. Hugging and sniffing and snuggling. There was a little damp patch seeping through my curls.

'Your tears are dripping on my head!' I mumbled.

'Yours are making my shoulder all soggy,' Cam sniffed.

'I'm not crying. It's hay fever,' I insisted.

'Idiot!' said Cam, hugging me harder.

'I thought you'd be really really cross with me.'

'I *am* really really cross,' Cam said fondly. 'Where have you *been*? Elaine and I have been going frantic ever since your mum rang to say you'd done a bunk. The police are out looking for you, I hope you realize.'

'Wow! What about telling the telly people? I hope I'm on the news. Can we video it?'

'I'd better phone everyone in a minute to say you're safe. So what happened, Tracy? Your mum said she thought everything was fine. She's very upset.'

'She couldn't wait to get shot of me!'

'That's not true. She really cares about you. You know she does. Look at all the presents.'

'Yeah. The presents. The doll and the chocolates and all that other stuff I didn't want.'

'It looks like you got some seriously cool combat trousers from her,' said Cam, holding me at arm's length and admiring my legs.

'I know. I like the clothes OK. And she was fun some of the time. She dressed me up in her stuff and it was great. But then she got fed up. She got fed up with *me*. She left me on my own while she went out drinking.'

'She shouldn't have done that,' said Cam, cuddling me close again. 'Was that when you ran away?'

'No, I cleared off this morning. She couldn't wait to get rid of me, Cam, really. So I thought I'd do her a favour and push off out of it.'

'And worry us all silly. Where did you *go*?'

'I got the train back.'

'Yes, OK, but where have you been all day? I've been round and round the town looking for you in the shops and McDonald's and everywhere I could think of. I even went to the school.'

'Are you crazy? As if I'd ever go there!'

'Well, where did you go then?' Cam put her hand under my chin so that I had to look up at her. 'Tell me, Tracy.'

I suddenly *wanted* to tell her. 'There's this house I go to. I've been there lots of times. When I should be at school, only don't get mad at me. I see some people there.'

All sorts of expressions were flickering across Cam's face as if she was a human kaleidoscope. 'Which house? Which people?' she said, struggling to sound casual, though her fingers were digging right into my shoulders.

'It's an empty house. No-one lives there. But these boys sometimes go there too. Alexander and Football. They're OK. They're my mates. Hey, they both want to be my boyfriend!'

'You're a bit young for boyfriends, aren't you, Tracy?'

'If you could see Alexander you wouldn't worry about him! And I can manage Football OK. Easy-peasy.'

'Do they go to your school?'

'Nope. Football's older – and Alexander goes to this posh all-boys place.'

'But they bunk off too?'

'Well, Football's excluded, so he can't go to school even if he wants. And Alexander's going to go back to his school now because he's decided he needs to do well in his exams.'

'Good for Alexander! So what are you going to do, Tracy? Get yourself excluded from school altogether or go back and try hard?'

'It's not like I've got a real choice. Alexander's an old brainy box, top of everything.'

'You've got a brainbox inside here too, you know,' said Cam, gently tapping me on the top of my head with her fist.

'Oh *sure* – and Mrs Vomit Bagley's going to make me her little teacher's pet and all the kids will want me to be their best friend?' I said sarcastically.

'You won't be in Mrs Bagley's class for ever. And it sounds as if you've got the knack of making friends now. But if you really hate this school we'll try again to get you in somewhere else. Liz says she might be able to get you into her school.'

'I bet she wouldn't half boss me about if she was my teacher.'

'You *need* bossing about. You're the naughtiest kid I know.'

'But you still want me back?'

'You know I do.'

'Even after all the stuff I said?'

'I said stuff too. But that's OK. People who love each other are allowed to have quarrels.'

'Love?' I said, my heart going thump thump thump.

'I love you,' said Cam.

My heart shone scarlet like a Valentine. 'No-one's ever loved me before.'

'Your mum loves you too,' said Cam. 'Maybe she's changed her mind about having you back on a permanent basis, but I'm sure she'll want to keep in touch.'

'Or maybe she'll wait another five years,' I said. 'We'll see. I don't care. I'll be OK with you, Cam. If that's what you really want.'

'Is it what you want, Tracy?'

'You know it is.'

I looked all round me. We were still in the hall. I looked down at the dingy bare floorboards and up at the grubby ceiling and around at the tattered posters on the walls. 'Though we could get this old dump smartened up a bit,' I said. 'Seeing as it's my home too. We could get a proper carpet for a start.'

'Maybe a rug,' said Cam. 'We could make one together, you and me.'

'And paint the walls something bright. Red!'

'Something subtle. Claret? Burgundy? Let's have a drink to celebrate your homecoming. Red wine for me, Coke for you, right?' Cam put her arm round my shoulders and we walked towards the kitchen.

'We could have new posters. You could choose. *Bright* ones,' Cam offered, resticking a tattered corner to the wall with a blutack blob.

I concentrated on the picture. There was a great big beach with a piano stuck on the sand with a little girl sitting on top, and a woman in a long dress and bonnet by her side.

'Why have they got a piano on the sand?'

'It's from a film. My favourite. About this mother and daughter. I've got it on video. Do you want to watch it?'

So we watch it together.

240

And the next day we got to watch *my* favourite film together.

There's no place like home. Well, most of the time. Cam and I still have mega-arguments sometimes.

Lots of times.

But then we make up.

We have great times together. Cam cooks me special treats.

Sometimes I cook her special treats too.

We work together and go out together and

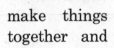

make things together and

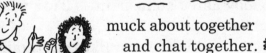

muck about together and chat together.

Of course we can't do everything together. I have to go to school, worse luck, worse luck, worse luck. I *might* be able to switch to Liz's school at the end of this term but till then I'm stuck with Mrs Vomit Bagley and Roxanne and all her putrid pals and even though this is a Happy Ever After ending Mrs V.B. is still the Wicked Witch and Roxanne is that weirdo princess that spews up toads and frogs every time she talks.

Mr Hatherway is all right though.

I've made a new friend at school too. He's called Trevor and he's the smallest boy in Year Three and everyone picks on him. (He's the one who had the nose-bleed, remember?) Mr Hatherway asked if I'd keep an eye on him in the playground. So I do. Nobody dares go near little Trev when *I'm* around.

I think Trevor likes me, though he doesn't say much.

I know Alexander likes me – and he says lots and lots. I've been to his house again. I ate all my tea this time, and had a second and then a third helping of cake. Alexander's been to my house too. Alexander had a great time. He and Cam had this long long long discussion about books.

Alexander likes Cam a lot. But he likes me more.

I think Football likes me the most though. I don't go round to his house much but he comes round to my house lots. We play football, surprise surprise. Out in the yard. Sometimes Cam plays too. And Jane and Liz. You'll never guess what. Jane is brilliant at football, even though she's so big. She's better than Alexander's dad. Even better than Football himself. Though he won't admit it. He's working on his game. Alexander's dad has got him into this club. I'm not sure how long this will last. Football hasn't got the knack of getting on with people. He's had a few arguments already. He might find he gets excluded. But I'm never going to exclude him. He can stay my friend no matter what.

I think he still sometimes hangs out at the empty house. Alexander doesn't go there any more. I don't either. Though I took Cam there once.

I made out it was *my* home and I showed her all round. Most of Alexander's cardboard furniture got broken up and so the house looked a bit sad and empty and dirty.

'But I could make it look really great,' I said, taking Cam by the hand and leading her around the living room. 'Maybe I could live in this house when I'm grown up, right? I'll have a chandelier and a ruby-red carpet and a big squashy sofa and a telly as big as the wall. I'll stay up half the night watching telly and then sleep really late and then I'll do a bit of work. I'll write these best-selling books, OK? And then I'll stop writing around five and have tea. I'll have a big birthday cake every single day.'

'You'll get pretty tubby then,' said Cam, poking me in the tummy.

'I won't eat it all by myself. I'll share it. I'll invite Alexander round. He can pop in between his brain surgery operations. And I want Football to come too, though he'd better not eat too much birthday cake if he's in serious training. And guess who else I'll invite?' I paused.

'Mrs Vomit Bagley?' said Cam.

'*No* chance!'

'Elaine?'

'Maybe. Once in a while, for old time's sake. No, someone else. Someone important.'

'Your mum?'

'If she'd come. I wouldn't bank on it though. Come on, Cam, *guess*!'

'I haven't a clue,' said Cam, but she was looking hopeful.

'YOU!' I said, and we had a big hug.

ABOUT THE AUTHOR

JACQUELINE WILSON is one of Britain's most outstanding writers for young readers. She is the most borrowed author from British libraries and has sold over 20 million books in this country. As a child, she always wanted to be a writer and wrote her first 'novel' when she was nine, filling countless exercise books as she grew up. She started work at a publishing company and then went on to work as a journalist on *Jackie* magazine (which was named after her) before turning to writing fiction full-time.

Jacqueline has been honoured with many of the UK's top awards for children's books, including the Guardian Children's Fiction Award, the Smarties Prize, the Red House Book Award and the Children's Book of the Year. She was awarded an OBE in 2002 and is the Children's Laureate for 2005-2007.

ABOUT THE ILLUSTRATOR

NICK SHARRATT knew from an early age that he wanted to use his drawing skills as his career, so he went to Manchester Polytechnic to do an Art Foundation course. He followed this up with a BA (Hons) in Graphic Design at St Martin's School of Art in London from 1981-1984.

Since graduating, Nick has been working full-time as an illustrator for children's books, publishers and a wide range of magazines. His brilliant illustrations have brought to life many books, most notably the titles by Jacqueline Wilson.

Nick also writes books as well as illustrating them.

STARRING TRACY BEAKER

Jacqueline Wilson

Illustrated by Nick Sharratt

Tracy Beaker is back . . . and she's just desperate
for a role in her school play. They're performing
A Christmas Carol and for one extremely worrying
moment, the irrepressible Tracy thinks she might not
even get to play one of the unnamed street urchins.
But then she is cast in the main role. Can she manage
to act grumpy, difficult and sulky enough to play
Ebenezer Scrooge? Well, she does have a bit of help on
that front from Justine Pain-In-The-Bum Littlewood . . .

As Tracy prepares for her big moment, Cam is the one
helping her learn her lines. But all Tracy really wants to
know is if her film-star mum will make it back from
Hollywood in time to watch her in her starring role?

This hilarious and heartbreaking new story from the
bestselling, award-winning, Jacqueline Wilson, follows
her most popular character through ups and downs,
laughs and tears. Fifteen years on from her first
appearance on the page, Tracy Beaker is as vibrant
and entertaining as ever.

DOUBLEDAY
0 385 61017 3
978 0 385 61017 9

CANDYFLOSS
Jacqueline Wilson

Floss loves spending weekends with her dad in his
greasy spoon café, even if it isn't the smartest place in
town and only has three regular customers. Even
Floss's best friend Rhiannon turns her nose up at it.
When Floss's mum and her new husband Steve move
to Australia, Floss faces a difficult choice – but decides
to stay at home with Dad. He's not much good at
ironing school clothes or putting up garden swings,
but they muddle along happily on a diet of chip
butties and candyfloss from the local funfair. But then
disaster strikes and they find themselves homeless.
Will their new fairground friends help out? Could
Dad and Floss be destined for a life on the road?

A wonderfully moving and brilliantly entertaining
story of family life from the Children's Laureate,
Jacqueline Wilson.

ISBN 0 385 60837 3

CLEAN BREAK

Jacqueline Wilson

When Dad and Mum break up, Em does her
best to cheer up her little brother and sister, even
though she's miserable too. She dances around
and tells wonderful tales all about their favourite
glove puppet. Em knows how a good story can
make life seem better. She is always cheered
up by reading one of her favourite books. If Em
got to meet the author, it would be a dream
come true. But could her other greatest wish
be granted? Is any story powerful enough
to bring Dad back?

Another wonderful book about real family life
from a prize-winning, best-selling author.

ISBN 0 440 86643 X

MIDNIGHT

Jacqueline Wilson

*Fairies steal away beloved babies and leave
a changeling in their place...*

Violet has always been in the shadow of her
mesmerising, controlling brother Will – by turns
delightful and terrifying. But now Will has learned
a shocking secret about his own past, and things
seem to be getting worse. Violet retreats into her
fantasies based on the fairy characters created
by her absolute favourite author, Casper Dream.

The arrival of Jasmine, a new girl at school who
immediately befriends Violet, seems like it might
change Violet's life for the better. Will Jasmine
allow her to break free of Will's spell?

A magical and atmospheric novel from
multi-award winner Jacqueline Wilson.

ISBN 0 440 86578 6

BEST FRIENDS

Jacqueline Wilson

*Alice is my very best friend. I don't know
what I'd do without her.*

Gemma and Alice have been best friends since they
were born. It never seems to matter that Gemma
loves football while Alice prefers drawing or that
Gemma never stops talking while Alice is more likely
to be listening. They share everything. Then one
day Gemma finds out that there's something Alice
isn't sharing. A Secret. And when Gemma discovers
what it is, she isn't sure if she and Alice can
stay Best Friends Forever . . .

A delightfully touching and entertaining story
from a best-selling, prize-winning author.

'A true children's writing genius'
Good Book Guide

ISBN 0 440 86579 4